Fighting Evil

Asmodais and the Vatican Elite Force

Bradley Rae James

iUniverse, Inc.
New York Bloomington

Fighting Evil
Asmodais and the Vatican Elite Force

iUniverse books may be ordered through booksellers or by contacting:

iUniverse
1663 Liberty Drive
Bloomington, IN 47403
www.iuniverse.com
1-800-Authors (1-800-288-4677)

Because of the dynamic nature of the Internet, any Web addresses or links contained in this book may have changed since publication and may no longer be valid. The views expressed in this work are solely those of the author and do not necessarily reflect the views of the publisher, and the publisher hereby disclaims any responsibility for them.

ISBN: 978-1-4401-9433-7 (sc)
ISBN: 978-1-4401-9435-1 (dj)
ISBN: 978-1-4401-9434-4 (ebk)

Printed in the United States of America

iUniverse rev. date: 2/5/2010

The Prologue

In the days before humans, the Creator made two forces to test on his newly manufactured universe. He created the angels, who became his obedient servants at conception. Angels could not disobey the Creator himself because their ability to choose right from wrong was not inbred into their makeup. The second group was formed of smokeless fire. They were called jinns, and the Creator used them to populate the newly formed planet. He gave the jinns dominion over every living creature. Since the jinns were made in his image and he expected them to grow based upon his beliefs, he gave them the ability to make decisions and to rule on Earth. The jinns were given unlimited power to control their destiny. The Creator was pleased with the jinns, so he rested.

The jinns, following the example of the Creator, established their own rules and their own realms of influence, and those jinns who did not abide by the commands of the group in power were often slain by the armies of the controlling jinns. Wars were inevitable, and strife was the norm of the period.

After a while the Creator returned to the world he had created and was not pleased with the development of the jinns. Their evolution had been too quick, and their motives and actions were not for the benefit of his other creations. He decided that he would create another group of beings that would not so be aggressive or powerful. The new creatures would need to be more like the angels but would have the ability to think and make decisions on their own. He would not make the same mistake with the new creation and would limit the power and the knowledge of the new beings. The new creatures would evolve over time and would not be given the keys to the universe until they had earned them.

The creator used clay and water to fashion a being whom he called Adam. He placed Adam in a very secure location in a spot that he had designated the Garden of Eden. It was far away from the jinns. There God gave Adam the simple job of naming all the animals he had created. It was a simple task, but once Adam completed it, the human could evolve in a more secure framework.

The jinns quickly became aware of the new entity. Jealous by nature, they quickly grew jealous of Adam. They argued among themselves about who would take control of the new "animal" after the Creator went away again. The self-proclaimed King of the Jinns, Iblis, decided that the new creature was in the likeness of the Creator; because the Creator had given the jinns dominion over the other creatures, the human should fall under jinn control too. Iblis spoke to the Creator and offered to supply companionship for the new animal. The Creator was swayed by the words of Iblis and allowed the jinn to supply female companionship to Adam.

Iblis created a small village outside the Garden of Eden and named the place Nod. He then ordered one of his slave female demons, Lilith, to take Adam and teach him the meaning of sex and how to procreate. Lilith was not overly pleased to be sent to couple with this creature of an inferior species, but she obeyed her master. She did not wish to be alone with the "animal" for any length of time, so she brought her sister, Naamah, with her to meet Adam.

Lilith and Naamah, accustomed to powerful jinn males, were dismayed at the weakness of the new animal. Adam did not have the strength or sexual prowess of a jinn male. He was a neophyte when it came to sex. Both female demons produced a son through Adam, and fortunately the boys had more jinn traits than human traits.

Naamah named her son Asmodais and immediately took the boy to live with the jinn. The son was handsome, with black hair and dark skin. He had good manners and an engaging nature. As he grew older, Naamah noticed that other female jinns were attracted to him in a lustful way. He did not care to settle down with just any one female, which had been the rule applied to the Jinns who followed Iblis. Iblis noticed this trait in Asmodais too and soon was calling Asmodais the Prince of Lust.

The Creator, noting that Adam was having difficulty mating with the jinn females, created a more docile mate for Adam. He placed the female, Eve, in the Garden of Eden with Adam and forbade the jinn females to visit Adam in the future. The Creator watched as Adam and Eve grew in their love for him. The Creator was proud of his new beings and named them humans.

The Creator called the jinns together and proclaimed that the human species would replace the jinns as the dominant species on the planet and that all his creations would serve the humans. The jinns were taken aback by this decision of the Creator. They could not believe the Creator would subjugate them to this lesser animal. Iblis stood before the mighty Creator and argued for his realm, stating it was wrong for an animal made of clay to have dominion over the jinns, who were created from fire and smoke. He asked why that one such animal should be able to control so many legions of jinns. The Creator dismissed the argument and banned the jinns to a realm apart from that of humans. Again eloquently, Iblis argued for the jinns' continued existence on the Earth that had been theirs for so many centuries. The Creator then made a decision that the jinns could remain on Earth but could not hamper the evolution of the human species. The jinns should remain separate throughout eternity from the humans.

Iblis argued that the new animals would serve the Creator better if they could be taught the ways of the jinns, and their evolution could proceed more rapidly through direct interaction with a much more powerful race of beings. The Creator accepted no part of this last argument and closed the conference.

Iblis was not pleased with the decision of the Creator, to say the least. If Adam and Eve could reproduce, then the realm of the jinn would soon be reduced. Adam had created sons with Lilith and Naamah, so there was no reason to believe that Adam would not be able to beget children with Eve. Unfortunately for the jinns, Adam was protected by the barriers of the Garden of Eden, and no female jinns were allowed into the garden. So Iblis sent Lucifer, his most eloquent womanizer, to visit the human woman. He did not know what Lucifer did to the woman, but he must have tempted her very effectively. A few days later, Iblis discovered that the Garden of Eden had disappeared, and Adam and Eve were alone in the world of the jinns.

Iblis requested an audience with the Creator again. He proposed to assist the humans in withstanding the world where they now found themselves. The Creator was upset with Adam, so he listened to Iblis's proposal that the jinns would honor the humans as a separate species, albeit an inferior species, and provide guidance for their growth and maturity. For their supportive role, the jinns would want a certain number of the humans as servants.

The Creator mulled over the new request from Iblis. The humans were weaker than the jinns but would survive with proper guidance. It would take years, even centuries, before the population of humans would be sufficient to tend to the requirement of the governing themselves and making a positive contribution to the developmental plans for the Earth. But the Creator was certain that the jinns would deter the evolution of the humans. The Creator wanted to deny the request, but he listened to Iblis. Iblis stated that there would always be more humans faithful to the Creator than to the jinns, and only those humans who decided to join the jinns would follow the jinns. Saintly humans, designated by the Creator, would never be tempted to join the jinns. But Iblis stipulated that when the end of time approached, those humans who followed the ways of the jinns would remain with the jinns for eternity. One final stipulation was that the Creator would not punish the jinns for seeking humans to join their realm. Reluctantly the Creator agreed to the conditions.

Adam and Eve begat sons, and the sons took female jinns as wives to continue the population of their species. The Creator altered the dominant genes of the humans so that interaction with the jinn females would produce only human offspring. Once enough female humans had been born into the human world, the use of jinns to reproduce dwindled. The Creator was happy with the development of humans with humans.

Centuries passed, and the followers of the jinns dwindled. Iblis and his followers began to note the change in numbers of their human slaves and the humans coming over to the jinn side of the equation. Iblis summoned his minions and ordered them to step up the process of human collection. He specified quotas and timeframes for the increase. He specified direct contact with humans; tempting them was mandatory. He reiterated the deal that he had made with the Creator: the humans must be allowed to choose who to follow. He wanted them to choose the jinns. He ordered his followers to do whatever it took to get new followers. Iblis singled out Asmodais, the Prince of Lust, and ordered him to increase his quota. Humans had received the sexuality trait from the jinns, which had made the humans more sexually oriented. Iblis recognized, although the promises of wealth and fortune were powerful inducements to join the jinns, that the lure of sexual misconduct would be the quickest method of attracting humans to the jinns. Iblis elevated Asmodais and gave him complete control over the collection of humans through sexual orientation.

The Creator had not been idle during this period of time. He had created religions among the humans to counteract the jinns. He made laws for his followers and stiff penalties for disobedience. At this point, the Creator termed the jinns evil and his other creations good.

It was in the Christian era, under the control of the Vatican, around 900 AD, that a special group of Christian militants was formed to combat the evil of that period. This group was trained in rooting out evil and destroying it. At the time of the creation of the team there was no difference between Church and State. The Church considered itself the State. The militants enjoyed autonomy and only reported directly to the pope. Their mission was to rid the world of demons and followers of evil. They were exonerated from the consequences of their actions by local laws and governing groups which were controlled by the Church. The initial inductees into this force were highly trained deacons with specialized assassin talents. As the world changed and the separation of Church and State became much more the vogue, the Church became aware of the militants being recognized as a terrorist organization. In the 1940s the Vatican aligned themselves with the International Police Organization, Interpol, which had been founded in 1923. Interpol, created in 1923, facilitates cross-border police co-operation and supports and assists all organizations, authorities, and services whose mission is to prevent or combat international crime. Interpol aims to facilitate international police co-operation even where diplomatic relations do not exist between particular countries. Action is taken within the limits of existing laws in different countries and in the spirit of the Universal Declaration of Human Rights. The militants were renamed the Vatican Elite Force and attached to a branch of Interpol but still remained a direct support arm of the Vatican. The Vatican had an easy task of equating international crime to crimes created by demons. Interpol bought the difference.

To support the new force the Vatican searched within its ranks to find qualified members to work for the new elite force. In the past they had used deacons to perform the role of assassins, but these people proved to be for the most part mercenaries with little direct support from the Vatican. These people were hard to control and often became corrupt. It appeared that the men were not immune from the demons. The Vatican began to search its ranks for priests that had proved themselves dedicated to the mission of the Church. These men were brought to the Vatican and trained to identify and root out evil. They were given extensive training in assassination techniques and the use of tools that would rid the world of evil. The Vatican was aware of the outside world identifying the group as a possible terrorist organization, so they worked with other religious sects to arrange for asylum for their team. The only way the acceptance could be granted was to rename these special priests to be called Deacons While performing religious services, they could affix the title *Father* to their name, but when exercising their rights of a VEF agent, they were referred to as Deacons. After many years of working with the governing bodies through the Interpol connection, the Vatican Elite Force was recognized as a true entity against evil.

While the members of the Vatican Elite Force had passed all the phases to become priests, once they became members of the elite team, the title of priest was honorary. They were truly no longer priests. They were specialized deacons of the Church. They could retain the term *priest* for official leverage with the Church and the world, but they were not restricted to strict adherence to priest rules.

Here this story begins. Deacon Domenico Marsala, the top agent of the Vatican Elite Force, has been sent to America to thwart the obvious sexual control of Asmodais Winters, believed to be a follower of Iblis and Asmodais. Marsala had successfully completed twenty-two assignments in his brief history with the VEF, and there was no reason to believe he would fail in this mission. Although in the past his targets had been primarily humans who had become followers of Iblis or some lesser jinn, he had worked directly against a number of demons and had curtailed their advancement. He had even trapped the homosexual demon, Sitri, and placed him in the catacombs of the Vatican. He was well-qualified and trained for fighting Asmodais Winters.

Asmodais Winters Comes to America

Asmodais, who used the human name Asmodais Winters, stared out the window of the airplane at the formation of the clouds. He enjoyed being in the human form. It gave him more opportunity to work his jinn magic on humans. Sure it limited his movement to standard modes of travel but that was okay with him. Also a factor was that without being inside this frail body he would need other bodies stretched throughout the world to jump into at a moment's notice. He could do that but there was little fun in doing it. He thought he could see Iblis, his king, staring back at him in the clouds. Iblis hated the human form and had demanded the jinns not take up the lesser form. Asmodais was not a minor jinn. He didn't share all the rules and regulations demanded by Iblis. He was his own jinn, period. He did not doubt that Iblis was paying attention to this mission. Iblis was not a trusting jinn. In truth, Iblis was a domineering control freak. He was more concerned with numbers than methods. This mission was critical to Iblis. The American people had been neglected far too long, and it was time to reunite the people with the strength and power of the jinns. In Asmodais's last venture to America twenty years earlier, he had sired many half-jinn children on human females, and by now these children should be growing up and showing their special abilities. Asmodais would check on those seeds and sow more. Iblis would be proud of the new followers and the potential for more followers.

Asmodais turned his eyes from the clouds to the first-class section of the airplane. There were twelve seats in the area, two rows of seats in the left, two in the middle, and two on the right. The area was large enough for another twenty seats, but passengers able to afford the luxury of first class should be better accommodated than those in business class or economy. With his vast fortune, he could definitely afford the higher fare.

The seat next to him was empty, but the other ten seats were occupied. Beside him in the middle seats were two men who were working on a speech for some large corporation. The older man was obviously the leader and did most of the talking. The other young man was busy taking notes on his laptop computer. Asmodais smiled when he thought of how Sitri, his homosexual peer, would enjoy making those two lovers.

Directly in front of him, in 1A and 1B, sat an elderly couple. The man was reading some novel, and she was knitting. He was at an exciting part of the book where the man was about to have sex with some young female client. Asmodais could picture the man turning the pages of the book to get to the sex scenes. The woman was thinking about some lover she had been with many years earlier and how much better off she would have been had she married that lover rather than the man next to her.

In 2A and 2B sat another elderly couple on their fortieth wedding anniversary. Their children had purchased this ticket to America for them. They held hands across the table between them. She was thinking of the children and how happy she was with them. He was thinking about the maid and hoping she would miss him while he was gone.

A young Chinese couple occupied 3A and 3B. He was going to America to continue his graduate work. She was happy to be with him and away from the Paris Chinese community. This was to be a fresh start for her. She was glad to be away from her overbearing French lover. She had not liked the Frenchman at all, but her husband was a full-time student, so she had had to earn money the only way she knew. She had told her husband that she was a waitress, and she did wait on tables at a famous Chinese restaurant in Paris, but she made most of her money with her body working at the hotel where the restaurant was located. She had provided room service for some of the wealthy male guests. It was not something she wanted her husband to know. She was certain he would never understand. She was correct in that thought.

The two in 3C and 3D were on their honeymoon. She was older than he was, but she didn't think he realized how much older. She had told him she was twenty-three, but she was twenty-nine. Asmodais wondered how long she expected to stay married to him if she had lied about her age from the beginning. The young man was nervous about returning to America with his French wife. He was from a small rural town, and his ex-girlfriend, whom he still e-mailed occasionally, wouldn't understand. Would she still talk to him? He would miss going to bed with her.

Asmodais closed his eyes to rest a few minutes. He wasn't tired; he just needed to concentrate. He knew the Vatican Elite Force would be sending an agent to follow him to America in hopes of destroying the human figure once and for all. Of course they would not succeed in America any more than they had been successful in Paris, but it would be interesting to see who they would actually send after him this time. He hoped they would send their best. The other four assassins had caused few problems to him and his staff. He'd really expected a better challenge from the mighty VEF.

A female voice interrupted his musing.

"How are you doing, Mr. Winters?"

He turned toward the voice and smiled up at the female stewardess as she eased down in the empty seat beside him. He was glad the seat had not been assigned. She was tall and slim, like most stewardesses he had known in his travelling experience. She had blonde hair, but he knew the hair had been dyed. She had been taught since she was young that blondes had more fun and were more enticing to the male population. She was wrong, but why should he correct her inane belief? She wore a loose blouse and a very short skirt. Both garments appeared to be of a no-wrinkle material. He knew the purpose of the uniform was not for enticement. Flight attendants are not supposed to come on to passengers and commonly dread passengers who come on to them. Their uniforms are meant to be neat and enduring, not seductive. But with his magic jinn facilities it was easy to persuade her to not only show off her lovely body but to break some of the classic attendant rules. She carried a tray and placed it close to her blouse, not wanting to distract him from her best asset, her long legs.

"I'm doing fine, and how are you, Alison?" He looked from her legs up to her face. He liked her pageboy coif and the round features of her face. He had read and memorized her name from her nametag when she had served him his first drink.

"Would you like another drink?" She turned toward him.

"You really don't think I need another drink, do you?"

"You've only had three drinks. You could probably handle a few more before we land. We still have another hour and forty minutes before we deplane at JFK," teasing him with her almost perfect smile.

"How would you like to go somewhere private with me?" Of course she would. He was flying first class and had paid for the extra service.

"Unfortunately, the flight attendant union frowns on those activities. It gives a bad name to our business," she said, rising from the chair.

He watched her move off. She hadn't said *no*, of course. No woman whom Asmodais wanted said *no* to him.

He glanced over at the honeymooners. They had just returned from the facilities near where they were seated. The woman had told the young man that she was glad he'd introduced her to the Mile-High Club. She was lying. She had been a member of that club for a number of years. He wondered whether he could seduce the young woman if her young groom were to go to sleep. He could force the man to take a nap if he really wanted her. It wouldn't take much to convince her to join him. He was the Prince of Lust, wasn't he?

He arose from his seat and moved toward the front of the airplane, exchanging a smile with both flight attendants. He slipped into the bathroom but did not shut or lock the door.

"Hi," Alison Cook whispered. She closed the door, so the light came on.

"I thought your union frowned on this kind of thing."

"Misty won't report me," she said as she began to unbutton her blouse.

He had been wrong about her. She wasn't as thin as he thought she would be, especially on top. She was more than a handful and much more than a mouthful. He knew that fact because he worked those breasts immediately.

Later as they were approaching Kennedy, Alison flopped down in the seat beside him and buckled in for the landing. She asked him if he had a place to stay for the night. He told her he would get a room at a local hotel, which was a lie. He knew his security would be at the airport waiting for him. She had smiled and asked him if he would like to spend the night with her in her apartment. She had a layover until the next afternoon. She had an apartment in Greenwich, Connecticut, that he could share with her for the night if he liked. He knew that Greenwich was not a bedroom community and there were very few rentals in that town. How could she afford an apartment in that area without a sugar-daddy supporting her? She probably did have someone helping her pay the rent. He knew it would drive his security forces bonkers, but this woman was too good to pass up. And since he was here to sow a few more seeds for Iblis, why not start with this lovely creature? He told her that he would be happy to spend the night with her.

Asmodais was carrying no luggage with him. His baggage had gone to his Winterhaven compound on an earlier flight. Twice he had flown and lost his luggage, and he wasn't ready to go through that experience again. He strolled casually through the crowds, his acute jinn vision taking in everything around him. Men and women glanced at the tall, dark man dressed in an equally dark suit. Most of them felt a flicker of attraction but moved away as he neared them, making sure he had an easy path through the concourse.

He spotted a young couple kissing and hugging in one of the alcoves. The young man, on his way to some war, was in uniform. He appeared tired from a long night of drinking and sex. He probably had a hangover. The young woman was clad in a very thin short dress. From the way they were plastered to each other, someone should have told them to get a room! The kiss was one that belonged to Bacall and Bogart, like Rhett and Scarlet. The young woman wanted to make sure that the kiss was on her soldier's mind for a very long time. Asmodais knew the man would be killed by a sniper within forty-eight hours of landing in the war zone, but he would say nothing to either of them to discourage the emotionally passionate moment. The young woman would mourn the soldier's death for a few hours then seek another man for a safe haven. She would never date another soldier.

The young woman's eyes opened as Asmodais approached. Then she closed her eyes and resumed the long kiss with the man at hand. Asmodais could have changed her life in an instant; he could have caused her to leave the doomed man and follow him, but at the moment he was not in the mood to collect her soul. There was just not enough time. He was certain that Iblis would collect her at a later date.

He stepped out into the afternoon sunlight. It was a beautiful April day, and he was ready to share the day with the world. Well, not all of the world but at least a few people occupying this part of it. He breathed in deeply, sucking the American air deep inside of his lungs. It was good to be back in the good old US of A after years away from this place.

A dark blue Porsche convertible came to a screeching stop at the curb directly in front of him. He smiled when he saw the blonde-haired stewardess beckoning him from behind the wheel of the automobile. The Porsche only confirmed she had a sugar-daddy to take care of her. She had rushed through customs to be there when he arrived at the baggage claim exit. Her timing could not have been better for him or for her. He slid into the passenger's seat. She sped away and merged into the Saturday afternoon traffic.

Alison Cook talked as fast as she drove her Porsche. She rambled about her fabulous car and the great time she had on the flight from Paris in the same sentence. She had not been so talkative during the flight.

He glanced down at her legs as the outside wind twice lifted the skirt of the uniform high enough that he could see those gorgeous thighs. She had smiled at him both times. If he'd asked her to pull over, she would have. However, he knew the Porsche would have been less convenient than the bathroom they had shared on the trip over. He allowed her to continue toward Greenwich at her rapid pace.

She pulled into an apartment complex in Greenwich in seventy-two minutes, then together they exited the small car. She rushed to her first-floor apartment and had the door opened by the time he reached the area. She stepped aside and let him enter first. She followed, making sure the entry was closed and locked.

The domicile was completely furnished by the landlord or her sugar-daddy and was very neat and orderly. She led him through each living space, rambling a mile a minute as she went from room to room. There was a kitchen and a dinette, very adequate for a single woman living alone. She had a small living room with a fully stocked bar. Behind the bar were small bottles of liquor one could obtain from the serving stewardesses, stashed in one corner. A large television was near an artificial fireplace. There was a two-person sofa, called a love seat, facing the television, and a large captain's chair that looked very comfortable. Pictures of airplanes adorned the three walls. There was a glass sliding door that opened to a small porch. He noticed through the thin curtain a George Foreman grill was sitting on a table on the porch.

Off the living room was the master bedroom with a king-sized bed and a small dresser filled with makeup and assorted sundries neatly placed. There were two doors off the master bedroom. One of the doors led to a full walk-in closet where she stashed her stewardess overnight bag for safe keeping. She would repack the bag before her next trip the following day. The second door led to her bathroom, which was a little larger than the bathroom on the airplane. However, it had all the necessities—a toilet, a sink with a mirror, and a glassed-in shower area large enough for two people to bathe together.

Asmodais thought the apartment looked like an expanded hotel room. It was very neat because she spent very little time here. As a jinn who doesn't need shelter the way humans do, the apartment didn't interest him that much. As a jinn in a human body the place was sufficient. He would have enjoyed seeing firelight and candles, perfumes, incense, and moonlight. But other than that he wasn't fussy or very concerned about the accoutrements.

The bachelorette apartment suited her life as a flight attendant who was rarely at home.

He could sense that she was nervous. She had brought him to her home as she had promised on the trip over, but she was unsure how to proceed. She was prepared to do whatever he wanted her to do but didn't know how to begin.

He asked her if she was a good cook, and she responded that she was an excellent cook. She asked him if he was hungry, and he told her he would be hungry later. She gave him her best smile. She knew what he meant by *later*.

She led him back to the bedroom with the king-sized bed. He followed her closely. Once they were both in the sleeping quarters, she walked away from him. He watched as she pulled down the white spread that covered the bed. He quickly noted the black silk sheets. He wondered how many men over the centuries had been seduced with black silk sheets. He wondered how many men she had seduced on those same sheets.

She turned to face him and began to ease off her uniform and let it drop to the floor. She retrieved the uniform and folded it neatly and placed it on the edge of the vanity. She was wearing no panties or bra because both had been removed in the airplane and stowed in her carrying case and she had not put them back on. She eased out of her flat shoes and stood completely naked in front of him.

"You are very beautiful," he said as he backed up and took in the full view of her naked body. He had visualized her without clothes and his vision, as usual, had been perfect.

"I want to be beautiful for you. I want you to want me," she whispered.

She could look young and naïve, as if this were the first time she'd entertained a man. An attendant with a Porsche and an apartment in Greenwich had obviously entertained men. She eased down on the edge of the bed and stared up at him. He smiled when he saw how the black silk sheets accentuated her young, vibrant, tanned body. Then he began to undress in front of her while she watched from the edge of the bed.

Once he was nude, he eased down and sat on the bed beside her.

"Do you like it rough or gentle?" The Prince of Lust could go either way. Most women would say *gentle*, but their animal instincts would take over in the actual deed, and the roughness always prevailed.

"Master, my body is for you. I'll serve as you so desire," she responded. She climbed further onto the bed and stretched out.

So she already recognized him as her master. That was a good sign. This one was going to be a good conquest for Iblis and for his own satisfaction. He mounted her; she wrapped those long legs around him. A few seconds later, he entered her, and she immediately moaned.

He smiled down at her. He knew he could destroy her if he wished or at least destroy her for other men. She had been kind to him. He would allow her to survive. She would be a great conquest to add to his family.

Deacon Marsala Reaches America

Deacon Domenico Marsala had not been to America in years, but he had heard that Asmodais Winters had flown to America from France. The Vatican Elite Force had been notified of the trip, so they sent their number-one assassin to take care of the potential problem. Marsala had been on twenty-two missions for the Vatican Elite Force and had never failed. He had no reason to believe he would fail this mission. He was on a mission blessed by the Pope and God. Therefore, he knew that he would succeed.

Asmodais Winters had eluded the Vatican Elite Force in France due to the security measures supporting the head of a large company. Four agents had failed to assassinate the man in France and had ended up dead. However, in America, the security would not be nearly as good. Things were looking up for Deacon Marsala. Now it was up to him to execute his plan.

Marsala appeared to be in his late fifties, but he was strong and fit. He was a little over six feet tall and weighed approximately 180 pounds. He still had a full head of hair. Many had compared him to the mature Clark Gable. He thought he looked more like Omar Sharif, only without the beard.

Marsala was met at the airport by Bishop Robert Davies from the archdiocese of Hartford, Connecticut, in a stretch limo. Bishop Davies had been ordered by the Vatican to give him whatever support he required. The bishop appeared to be an older man, perhaps in his late sixties. He was gray-haired and a little overweight. His profitable life as a bishop had paid off for Davies.

Davies reported that Asmodais Winters had arrived on the Paris flight and had been driven away by a stewardess who lived in Greenwich, Connecticut. His spies believed Asmodais Winters was still with the woman. Marsala requested a car and the address of the stewardess. Davies promised him any support he needed. The bishop also noted that his intelligence had reported that Asmodais had spent some time in Stamford twenty years ago, and that if history repeated itself, the man would be in Stamford the next day.

Marsala could not believe that Asmodais Winters would make a mistake so quickly after entering America. Why had Asmodais taken refuge with a young stewardess instead of seeking protection with his minions in America? Asmodais was no fool. He must know that the VEF would follow him to America. Four times the VEF assassins had tried to get him in Paris. Had he become complacent because he's unimpressed with their track record? Did Asmodais really believe that coming to America would be a relief? He did not believe it would end so quickly, but hope does spring eternal.

In ninety-eight minutes, the limo pulled into the drive at the rectory in Stamford. Nuns and priests gathered to greet the bishop and his guest. Deacon Marsala did not like the fanfare, but he knew the reception was not for him as much as for the bishop since everyone reported directly to the cleric. The bishop introduced him as a special envoy from the Pope and did not mention his affiliation with the secret Vatican Elite Force circle.

He had dinner with the bishop and went to Mass with him later. He prayed to God that this mission would be completed expeditiously. He found it interesting how the Mother Superior took note of Bishop Davies. Was there something going on between those two? Not that it mattered to him; he was on a specific mission and not a mission to resolve the issues of this Church.

He found the late-model Malibu supplied by the rectory to his liking, and with the GPS and the address of the stewardess, he drove to the apartment complex where she was hosting Asmodais Winters.

He sat outside in the parking lot surveying the territory for possible escape routes in case Asmodais Winters eluded him. There were very few escape routes except for the fire escape from the third floor, so he felt more comfortable. It was nearly ten o'clock at night. He considered moving quickly and attacking Asmodais without warning, then decided that attacking after midnight would be better. The death of Asmodais early on Easter Sunday would be perfect.

He remained in the vehicle and prayed for almost two hours for guidance and for a quick kill. In his twenty-two assignments, he had assassinated fifteen of the targets within the first twenty-four hours. Asmodais Winters appeared to be following the same pattern. It would be good to put this notch on his belt and fly back to Rome on Monday morning.

Asmodais Escapes

Asmodais received the warning call around ten o'clock that a man from the Vatican Elite Force had been seen at the Stamford Rectory. The man had been given a dark blue Malibu and had left the Rectory shortly after the nine o'clock Mass. The caller wanted to know if the assassin should be eliminated immediately. Asmodais told the caller to be on the alert but not to take any actions unless he specifically gave them orders to do so. He was not afraid of a single VEF agent and would not let the would-be killer disrupt the evening he had planned.

Asmodais stood at the living room window in the dark munching on a piece of southern-style fried chicken. The young stewardess had indeed been an excellent cook. They had supper with the woman in 301, Alison's friend who was entertaining a pilot Alison knew had been excellent. He had told the women that he might visit her later. When the woman had left he knew she hoped he would stop by that night. He was glad he hadn't destroyed Alison with sex before she made him dinner. Alison Cook joined him and handed him a glass of champagne. The low light from the bedroom backlit her. She was still naked. He had put his boxer shorts back on, but she had remained ready for anything he wanted. He knew she hoped that he would want her again before the night was over. He was determined to fulfill that need at least once more.

He peered through the thin curtains and spotted the Malibu in the parking lot. He smiled when he saw the man praying in the front seat. The man was obviously asking for guidance from God for a swift kill. He smiled too because he knew the man would wait until after midnight to attempt the assassination. Tomorrow was Easter Sunday, and God would obviously be on the assassins' side—or so the agent would believe. Did the Vatican Elite Force think killing him would be so easy after four unsuccessful tries? Did they believe that just because he was in America, he would be unprotected?

"Master, is there anything else I can do for you?" the young stewardess asked. Her innocent eyes begged him for another round.

He wiped his hands. This time he was gentle with her until the very end. She was prepared for his final deep thrust inside of her body. He had decided to make her pregnant, and whether she knew it or not, the seed was implanted deep inside her womb. The way she clung to him after the eruption, he knew she was well aware of the possible impregnation and was pleased to be carrying his child.

He left her sleeping contently on the bed. She had been a good conquest for him. She and their half-jinn child would always be at his disposal. He went to the living room and called his security people on his cell. He simply told them to pick him up in twenty minutes, when he left the complex. They had been told his arrival plans; they would know where he was.

Now he could see the man stirring in the car. It was twenty minutes to twelve. The man obviously didn't know Asmodais Winters was a true jinn. Otherwise, why would he wait until midnight to attack. This was when jinns were the strongest. It did make sense if he thought Asmodais was human. The man would be making his move very shortly. Asmodais knew it was time to leave the stewardess. He could simple surprise the agent by walking out the front door, but what fun would that be? The fire escape would be more interesting.

Asmodais left the apartment on the first floor and moved silently up to the third floor. He had noticed that the outside fire escape opened from number 301. He had planned to use that flight route if necessary. Now he knew this mode of departure was the only one available to him without killing the VEF spy. He knocked gently on the door and identified himself.

The same young woman that had shared dinner with him and Alison opened the door immediately. She was wearing a short night gown. She had been waiting for him to join her. He knew that no woman in her right mind would open a door to a stranger. But his jinn magic had caused her to drop her normal caution. Had he not been in the human form, he could have simply walked through the door, but the human form has limitation. She had dark hair with blonde streaks. She was shorter than Alison Cook, but her smile was just as interesting. From the flush of her cheeks, he knew that he had caught her in the midst of sexual activity. The men's clothing on the floor near her coffee table confirmed his suspicions.

"How can I assist you, Master?" she asked softly stepping to the side and encouraging him to enter the apartment. She eased the door closed after he passed her.

She offered no resistance when he cupped her face with his hands and kissed her gently. Her body melted against his body. He could feel her nudity beneath the gown. He wondered if he had her before, or possibly her mother or grandmother? She tasted familiar.

He calculated quickly. It would take the assassin a few minutes to complete his move. The agent would realize that his target had escaped through the fire escape. That would take another few seconds. If everything worked against him, Asmodais would still have approximately ten minutes before he had to be out of the complex. He reached for the woman and pulled her close to him. He did have a few extra minutes.

As she moved against him, she released the gown and it fell onto the floor behind her. The stewardess had a better body, but at the moment, his eyes were only on this woman. He pulled her into his arms and gave her another kiss. He didn't have time to do what he wanted with her, so instead he pressed her shoulders gently downward. She received the message very quickly as she began to immediately give him skillful oral sex. He could sense that she was not a novice in this mode. He wondered if her name was Monica.

Unfortunately his time was too limited for her to finish the task at hand. He forced himself to pull her to her feet. "Now go and finish this up with your friend," he ordered.

He went to the window leading to the fire escape and exited her apartment silently. He knew his dark clothes would conceal him from view by anyone below, except perhaps his security detail. He made his way silently down the metal stairs and ended up outside the building just as the agent was getting out of the Malibu.

He watched in the shadows as the man crossed the courtyard. The man used a tool to unlock the front door and then entered the apartment. This was the cue for Asmodais to make his move. He moved quickly to the Malibu and cut the back two tires with a long knife he always carried on him. He then stole silently into the cover of night.

One block from the complex, a stretch limo pulled up beside him. He immediately entered the limo. As soon as he was inside, the limo pulled into traffic.

He smiled at Angela Blanco across the seat from him. Angela Blanco was the executive secretary of his Winterhaven Security, a firm he had established twenty years earlier and funded from Europe.

"The Vatican Elite Force is at it again. They will never learn," he laughed softly, extending his hand to her. She took the hand and switched from her seat across from him to the bench next to him.

"This one is Deacon Domenico Marsala. He has a record of twenty-two confirmed assignments." She had done her homework.

"I have heard of him. It is too bad that his record will be tarnished, isn't it?" he said, placing an arm around her shoulders. She moved closer to him. She rested her head against his shoulder. He could smell her perfume. It was the same perfume she had wore in Paris the last time he had seen her.

"I heard you got married since the last time you were in Paris," moving a hand down the top of her opened blouse.

"Yes, Master, my husband is our top scientist. He is working on a new computer clone model that we hope to complete in a few days. Your timing in coming to America could not have been better," caressing the hand touching her breasts.

"Can he be trusted?" he asked.

"Yes, Master, I have complete control over him."

"How have you been?" he asked.

"Lonely, Master. My husband, although a brilliant scientist, does not have the proper skills to satisfy my needs—the needs that you, Master, taught me to have many years ago in Paris," cuddling even closer.

He was about to ask where they were going, but before he could request the information, the limo pulled into the driveway of a large mansion. She told him that the owner of the mansion was a devoted follower of his; the mansion would be a safe place for the evening.

The two exited the limo, and she led him to the front door where a man and woman were waiting. She had not re-buttoned her blouse. The man told Asmodais to consider the house his for as long as he needed it.

Asmodais barely glanced at the man. His interest was elsewhere—with the woman. From the jewelry around her neck, on her lobes, and on her fingers, she knew how to spend the older man's money. Her long hair flowed, in the Farrah Fawcett style, around her faultless face. She smiled. The silk charmeuse black robe flowed over the contours of her torso. The robe was open just enough in front to expose her ample breasts. Asmodais wondered if the woman had implants. If anyone could afford modifications to her body, this woman could. Her eyes moved to his eyes. Then she looked down immediately, submissively. The stewardess and Angela were beautiful, but this woman had the kind of beauty that only serious money could afford and maintain.

He reached out a hand to her, and she clasped it softly. He could feel the electricity pass between their bodies. She could feel it too. She looked at him as if the two of them were alone. She uttered only three words, so softly that he doubted anyone else, with the possible exception of Angela, could hear them. "Come with me."

The man said nothing as the woman led Asmodais into the house. A chandelier glinted above the broad stairs that wound upward to the second floor. She turned into the room on the right. It was the master bedroom. The room was carpeted with a fur rug. The whiteness of the rug made him think it was a polar bear rug. This suggested to him that the woman was very sensual and rather transgressive. It was the type of woman he preferred. The room was immaculate. He thought she would give the maids a raise tomorrow when they returned to clean the room. He walked to a large plate glass window and glanced outside. Beneath the room was a large Olympic swimming pool surrounded by several cabanas. He noted a wet bar near the pool. Even in the dark, he could tell that the grounds were well-kept.

He turned back to where she was standing. He spotted the large circular bed and a huge television across the room from it. He smiled. He knew she was from old money, and old money normally have rather conservative decorative tastes. Old money go for quality, dignity, comfort, and lasting values in their furnishings, but this bed was more to her sensual tastes. He wondered how many of her neighbors had beds in their master bedrooms like this bed, probably only a few. There was an oval mirror over the bed to match the contours of the bed. She used a remote control and turned on the television. "My husband and I enjoy porno films while we have sex. I hope you don't mind," she said, smiling toward him. He was not interested in the movie, but he was interested in her. As he moved toward her, she eased seductively out of her gown, exposing her naked body.

He let her undress him.

Meanwhile Angela and the man walked to the large den. Angela knew she was not in the league sexually with the man's wife, but she was prepared to take care of him while her master took care of his wife.

"He is a strong individual." He poured her a glass of wine.

"Do you mind that he is enjoying your wife?" Angela sipped the wine. He had not poured a drink for himself.

"He is Asmodais, the Prince of Lust—how would I ever be able to compete with him or deny him the pleasures of my wife?" His eyes traveled over her body.

"When will your daughter be home?" she asked him.

"She is at the movies with one of her girlfriends. I expect her home by one o'clock," he responded.

"He will want her too," she said, calmly finishing her drink.

A young girl, sixteen years of age, entered the den. Angela could see the resemblance between the girl and her mother. "Is he here?" the girl asked.

"Yes, with your mother," the man said softly.

Angela thought he was hoping that the girl would not want to go upstairs and bother her mother and the guest. He was hoping that she could be spared the ordeal of the night. Angela could sense his love and devotion to his daughter, more so than with his wife.

The young girl spun around, skirt flaring. She made a hasty retreat from the den. Angela could not hear the girl ascend the stairs but knew she must have leaped them at least two at a time.

"Do you have problems with this?" Angela asked the man.

"No, he is the master. We are his servants. If he wants my wife and my daughter, then who am I to have a problem with anything? Will you be joining the orgy?" he asked.

"I will be joining them later, but first I think you need a reward for being faithful to the master," Angela said as she placed the empty glass on the wet bar and took his hand. He took her to one of the downstairs guest rooms. She only left after he'd fallen into contented sleep. Then she joined the trio in the master bedroom.

Asmodais and Angela left the following morning. He'd impregnated his hostess and her daughter during the night with half-jinn seeds. Iblis would be happy with his two new converts. He would have made Angela Blanco pregnant too, but he knew she was barren. It was good to be back in "the good old US of A." Iblis would be proud of his start. The first day in America, he had already made four conquests. He included the woman in 301 as a conquest too.

Deacon Marsala Misses the Target

As soon as he entered the small bachelorette apartment, Deacon Marsala knew that he had missed Asmodais. He could sense the man wasn't there. Quickly he ran back to his automobile, hoping beyond hope that what he thought might have happened had not occurred.

"Damn," he muttered to himself when he noticed that both of his back tires had been slashed. Asmodais had eluded him and delayed his search. How had he have been so careless? He called the rectory and told them to send someone to fix the tires of the car. After the call, he knew he had a lot of clean-up activity to perform. It wasn't enough that Asmodais had eluded him. The stench of Asmodais must be eradicated from this young stewardess before it was allowed to fester and grow.

He returned to the first-floor apartment. He found the young stewardess resting peacefully on the large bed. She was still naked. He stared at her body. He had no doubts that Asmodais had used her body over and over all afternoon, probably only moments earlier. A woman does not sleep that peacefully unless she has just enjoyed a very satisfying sexual encounter.

He doubted she knew where Asmodais had gone, but he had to find out. The only way he knew to get a valid response from a woman who had been used by the devil as a play toy was to cleanse her body with holy water. He knew that normal Catholic believers believe a drop of holy water on the forehead would be sufficient. It is held to be effective through numinous powers. Even in exorcisms, a priest does not undress the victim and put holy water on in other body areas. That action would be against Christian modesty and would expose the priest to temptations of whatever entity he hoped to exorcise. In the sacrament of extreme unction, different body zones are anointed, but nothing is done that invades privacy or offends the modesty of the person. But Deacon Marsala was no normal priest. He had been cleared to use holy water to the fullest intent of the situation. Dealing with demons for over twenty years had given him more experience than most Catholic priests. He knew when it was important to stretch the rules of using holy water, and he had no aversion to follow the methods he had been taught. The body was sacred and private until the point it had been used by a demon or a demon advocate for evil purposes. Her lovely body looked to him like she truly needed to be saved. Asmodais wouldn't just let her live unless he had further plans for her. Those plans had to be nipped in the bud immediately. He reached into his coat pocket and retrieved a flask of holy water.

He slowly eased down on the bed near her waist. She stirred but did not awaken when he dripped holy water on her forehead. Still she made no movement beneath him as he used his fingers to spread the water on her breasts where he could still see the imprints of where Asmodais had bitten her.

With a swift motion, he poured the water between her thighs, and with his fingers, he forced the water even deeper inside her. The movement and the power of his stroke brought reality to the young beautiful woman abruptly.

"I am here to save you," he whispered to her, hoping she would comprehend his intentions.

"If you believe you're going to save me with water down there, then you are mistaken. The Master has enjoyed me to the fullest. I'm carrying his seed," she sneered at him, struggling to be free of him.

His attempt at saving her fell short when she twisted and kicked the bottle of water from his hands. She laughed at him.

"My body is his body," she screamed. It was the last time she would ever laugh or scream at anyone. Asmodais had corrupted her beyond his ability to save her. Even his holy water would not have been able to cleanse her body on the inside, especially if Asmodais had gotten her with-child. Unfortunately he had only one alternative left. He could not have her spreading Asmodais's evil to other parts of the world. No, this had to be terminated quickly. With a quick flick of her neck with his strong hands, she was silenced forever. He had not wanted to kill her. He had wanted to save her, but that was not to be. He stared at her lifeless body, and a tear flowed down his cheek. Human life was sacred to him and to the Church. Asmodais had left him no choice.

He arose and spread chrism, holy oil, on her forehead. Perhaps when she went to see the Almighty, he would see that she had been blessed and would take her into his family. If she went to the other place, then Iblis would leave her alone too, knowing that she had been blessed by holy oil.

He left her.

He climbed the stairs to the third floor, knowing the only way Asmodais could have eluded him was to use the metal fire escape. He knocked on the third-floor apartment door that led to the escape route. He needed to know if Asmodais had corrupted the person in that apartment too. He announced himself. She must have been expecting Asmodais to return because she opened the door immediately. One look at the young woman who opened the door, and he knew Asmodais had used her. But he could not have overused her as he had the woman from the first floor. She could possibly be saved.

He grabbed her by the head. Her lips were chapped and disfigured. He could smell the sour odor of her breath. He knew she had given Asmodais a different variety of sex, sex that was performed with the mouth. "Did he do more than let you give him oral sex?" he asked, holding her head still roughly by here streaked hair.

"No, there was no time," she responded, staring blankly up at him. She made no attempt to free herself. The power of God must be controlling this scene. Obviously Asmodais had not used his full influence on her in such a short time.

"Bring me a glass of wine" he ordered.

She obeyed without question. He quickly poured a drop of the holy water into the glass with the wine and told her to drink all of it. She downed the drink in one gulp.

He spotted the man's clothes on the floor near the sofa. He asked her if she had been with anyone else after being with Asmodais.

"I completed the method of sex started by him with my boyfriend. He is a pilot," she said, responding to his question.

She refilled the empty glass with wine, and after he poured more holy water into the glass, he told her to take it to her friend and make sure he drank it all. He followed her and watched as the man drank the full dosage of the mixture. Marsala poured a little of the holy water on both of their heads. He had been able to save them both with the concoction of wine and holy water. He was happy for them. They could not spread the contamination to others. It was unfortunate that he could not have saved the stewardess. He returned to his automobile by the fire escape route. Asmodais had been in America less than twelve hours, and he had already attempted to corrupt three people. The man had to be stopped, and he had to be stopped quickly.

While he waited for the repair truck, he began to think. Was Asmodais Winters a human at all? The research by the VEF command had documented that Asmodais Winters came from human parents, but could this documentation have been manufactured to cover the identify of Asmodais? The stewardess had been severely traumatized by Asmodais, to a point that she was willing to die for him. The woman upstairs, he was certain, had only spent a few minutes with Asmodais. Not a long time, but in those few minutes, Asmodais had worked his evil magic on her. She had given him sex. Asmodais had to know that when she gave him sex, she was committing herself to a life of evil. No human he knew had that much control over other humans. Perhaps this was how Asmodais had eluded the four assassins in Paris. Perhaps he wasn't human at all. If this was true, then his work was cut out for him over the next few days. Fighting the Asmodais, the Prince of Lust, was not something he looked forward to.

Once the car was repaired, he drove back to the Stamford rectory and obtained a room for the night. He was up in time for the early Mass, called matins, then returned to his quarters. He prayed most of the morning for God to give him guidance. It was not God's fault that he had not killed Asmodais. God had delivered Asmodais to him at ten o'clock at night. It had been his inaction that had allowed Asmodais to escape. In the future there must be no indecision on his part. When God delivered Asmodais to him again, he would not hesitate to kill him, if he could kill him.

Asmodais Goes to Mass

Asmodais Winters stood in the crowd of the Sunday Mass at the Stamford Catholic Church. He was standing in the rear of the auditorium with Angela Blanco on one side and a very attractive young woman on the other side. He generally enjoyed going to religious events, but at the Catholic Church, they were always inspiring, especially at Easter and Christmas. The people dressed up for the occasion and were always a little more friendly. Once they were open and friendly, corruption became much easier.

He glanced around the large congregation hall, noting the stained glass windows depicting the many deeds of the followers of Jesus, the son of the Creator. He wondered if these people would follow this Christian path if they really knew how many of those saintly figures had been followers of Iblis. Even Bishop Davies had not been spared from indoctrination into the Iblis family, and yet there the saintly man stood, watching over his masses.

Asmodais was in the back of the auditorium and could not see the faces of the women in front of him. He wondered how many in the congregation he had seeded on his last visit and how many of those offspring were at today's Mass. He smiled when he spotted the couple he had spent the night with in their mansion. Regal and well-dressed, they stood at the front. It was good to see his followers knew how to interact with others so well. The teenage girl, standing next to her mother, turned once and gave him a knowing smile, then returned her gaze toward the front of the auditorium. He was certain she would be about his business today.

He has loved this parish ever since his last visit here twenty years ago. There is major corruption in the parish: a bishop who molests acolytes, unchaste nuns, nuns who get pregnant. There's a reason for it, too: he is the reason for it. These humans are acting atypically. These humans are not in their right minds and haven't been for a long time. They are not free moral agents; they are ensorcelled; they are his puppets. They are being driven and used, not acting from their own convictions. This is a sick, bewitched parish. He wished all parishes were like this one clearly under siege, under paranormal influence—not a common or natural state of affairs in Catholic parishes. Iblis thought of this parish as a hallmark for the jinn way of life. That was the reason Asmodais had made a return visit to this part of the world.

Angela Blanco stood to his left with her husband. She was his servant. He had spent the night with her at the mansion and enjoyed renewing their relationship. The last time he had seen her was in Paris five years earlier, when she was working on a degree in business administration. It hadn't taken much to convince her to go to work for him in America. She was an American, and out of her general focus area in France. She had proven to be quite the administrator in his American ventures and quite the convert to him.

The young woman to his right was also known to him, although he had never met her personally. She was nineteen, almost twenty, and quite the looker. She had long red hair that fell over her shoulders and down to her hips. Today it was pulled back from her face in a ponytail. She was well-tanned from much time outdoors riding her favorite stallion, even in the winter months. It was a stallion her adopted father had given her at his expense three years earlier. She was not married, nor was she looking for a husband. The man on her right wanted to change her belief in marriage, but she had resisted him quite well. In fact, she was still a virgin, which was extremely rare these days in the teenage population around the world. A teenage girl who was past fifteen and still had her virginity intact was extremely rare. When the young woman smiled, you could only smile back at her. He thought of the young stewardess he had left the night before, but the thought was only fleeting; this woman far exceeded the stewardess in sheer female beauty. He could sense a strength about her that would test most human men.

He smiled at the teenage woman to his right. He wondered if she recognized him. He wondered if she had pictured him in her sleep. She was more than a half-jinn child. She had more of him than most young females. He waited until the bishop began to give his Easter spiel, then he mentally sent a message to both Angela and the young woman. He made them feel a warmth on their body and inside their body both above and below their waist. He knew better than to give them the illusion that he was a pervert, although he was certain Angela would approve of anything he wanted to do with her but the young woman would not understand the actions of a pervert. Angela Blanco stared straight ahead and made no indication that the sensations her body was feeling had any effect on her.

The young woman turned her head, smiled at him as though she recognized him.

He whispered to her, "Christ is risen indeed, my darling, and so am I."

She continued to smile then turned back toward the front of the crowded room. Asmodais now knew the young woman had dreamed about him often during her young life. She had been waiting patiently for his arrival. She had avoided contact with males because she was saving herself for him. He wondered how many sleepless nights she had spent thinking about him, thinking about having sex with him, thinking about this moment in time. He used his jinn magic to sexually stimulate the young woman even more. He used his jinn magic on both women as the bishop gave his oration. Neither woman offered any resistance to the probing thoughts.

Even though Asmodais was interested in the women beside him in the back of the church, he was equally interested in the nuns standing around the bishop as he delivered his speech. It had been twenty years since he had seen the nun whom he came to America to visit. He finally spotted her. She was the third woman on the back row toward the end. Her eyes were closed as she recited the ritual she had used so many times in the past.

He smiled to himself as he recalled his last visit with Sister Mary Alice. The convent knew her only as Sister Alice. She had been so young and so naïve in the ways of the world—taking her had been a real pleasure, even to him. He still could recall the visit after all these years. She was special. She had not been a convert to Iblis as Iblis had hoped, but she had often thought of him in her dreams. She would be his again.

He did catch her eye once when she opened her eyes for a moment. He knew she spotted him too, but she closed her eyes again. He could barely see her body through all her heavy habit, but he knew it must still be as lovely as it had been twenty years ago.

He spotted Deacon Domenico Marsala standing a few feet from the bishop. The man appeared to be a formidable opponent and very dedicated to God and to the Vatican. It was too bad he was on the wrong team. The VEF agent obviously did not recognize him.

He gently took a step backward until he felt the wall behind him at his back. The woman to his right moved backward too. He mentally moved a hand beneath her short skirt and stroked her bottom firmly. She wiggled gently but imperceptibly, trying not to alert the young man standing next to her. Angela Blanco turned to smile then turned back to the front. Angela would never interrupt him.

The young woman felt special as her body reacted to the touching of her body. She knew no human hands were touching her physically. He was doing this the same way he had done it in her dreams so many times n the past. God, how many times had she seen this man standing next to her in her bedroom? How many times had she offered her body to him? Life had been a struggle over the teenage years, wanting a man but saving her body for this man. This was the man she dreamed of. This is the man she wanted to bear a son for. This was the man that she would dedicate her life to. He was not touching her. He did not have to touch her to make his presence known and felt. The fact that he was standing beside her was good enough. The man on her right would never understand, but she really didn't care. The man on her left would be her introduction into womanhood. She had waited all these years for him to be the first. She would wait no longer. If he wanted her today, then she would give her body and soul to him today. Toward the end of the Mass, he whispered to her to meet him downstairs three minutes after the Mass was over. He mentally caused her to have a mild orgasm one more time; then he left her.

He descended the stairs in the vestibule of the church and found several rooms that were used for training. He didn't really care what the rooms were used for; he was going to use them for his own personal gain. He found a bathroom and wet some paper towels and brought them with him to a room. Four minutes later and exactly three minutes after the Mass ended, the young woman came to him. The couple never spoke to each other. She never cried out when he broke into her. He enjoyed having sex with her, and he knew she enjoyed it too. She used the wet towels to clean herself before she was ready to leave. When she left him, he gave her strict orders to not let her boyfriend touch her. She smiled as she left him.

He was about to leave the downstairs area when he heard a noise. He silently moved toward the sound. He came into the room where the head altar boy was changing his clothes. He smiled at the young boy and immediately brought him under his control. This was the bishop's favorite boy in this parish. He had control of the parish and had it for over twenty years. The boy smiled at him.

The young altar boy was found naked, twenty minutes later, comatose. Asmodais had ruined the altar boy for the bishop for that visit. He had taught the boy the difference between being with the bishop and being with a true demon. The boy had been delicious.

Sister Mary Alice

Sister Alice was extremely nervous; perspiration was flowing down her cheeks. For years she had dedicated herself to supporting the Church and its youth. It was her penance for sharing herself with Asmodais twenty years earlier. Why was he back? What did he want? She had seen him at the Easter Mass. She had wanted to yell to the bishop that the Lustful Evil One was in the audience, but she had remained silent. She had seen the handsome man leave the service and noticed the young woman who had been standing next to him leaving her boyfriend. She had observed the same young female ten minutes later with a very contented look on her face. She had no doubts that Asmodais had put that smile on the teenager's face. Had he known who the child was, then he might not have been so eager to do what he had done to the girl. Or perhaps that would not have mattered to him at all.

She had been on her way to prayers before the noon meal when she heard about the altar boy and the following ruckus that it caused. The boy seemed terrified. The parents were furious. Police cruisers had been dispatched to find the pervert. An ambulance and EMTs had taken the boy to Saint Joseph's Hospital for immediate attention. The church community was in a great turmoil. She did note that the bishop was calm through the entire ordeal. That was strange to her. She had no doubts that Asmodais had performed that evil deed too. She skipped lunch and went to her cell. She had told the Mother Superior that she needed quiet time to meditate and pray. Mother Superior had granted her request, as always.

Sister Alice knelt, silently praying from her prayer book and from her heart to be delivered from Asmodais. She was praying that he would bypass her and continue on his evil mission without seeing her. It was not long before she heard the light tap on her door. She knew who was coming to visit. She knew he would use the turmoil to conceal his entrance to the convent. With such a distraction, it would be easier for him to get to her without incident. She wanted to be so quiet that he would think she was not there and go away. But she knew he was back, and he was at her entryway wanting an audience with her. She knew that she would open the door and let him into her room the same way she had let him in her room twenty years earlier. Finally the Church lost, her faith lost, and she opened the door and went to her bed without even looking at him.

She stopped at the edge of the bed when she heard the door close and lock. In the last twenty-five years, that door had only been bolted shut once, and that was on his initial visit. She turned, and there he was, inches from her, wearing the same evil grin she had seen so many years earlier and so many times in her dreams.

She was tall for a woman, almost an inch over six feet, and thin at 140 pounds. She kept her long red hair hidden from the public; only a few of the nuns had ever seen her flaming red hair. She stood motionless and allowed his hands to gently remove her wimple. Her long, dark, red hair flowed to her shoulders as he began to straighten it out with his fingers.

"You are still as lovely as I remember," he whispered to her.

"I should be the same—because of you, I haven't aged a year in twenty years," she said sarcastically. "You don't know how hard it is to conceal your youth when all the others around you are aging." She was nervous at how easily he had taken control of her again.

"It was your choice to have my child and remain here. I offered to take you with me." Asmodais was still running his long fingers through the flaming strands.

"They took her away from me. I had to watch her grow up from afar," she said, keeping her head bowed, not looking up at him. She knew if she looked into his eyes, she would be as lost as she had been the last time she had been with him.

He explained calmly that she had known what would happen, years ago, if she didn't leave with him. It had been her choice to remain in the service of the Church. He had honored her request, and he had taken care of both her and her daughter over the years. She asked if he knew the young woman whom he had taken downstairs was his daughter. He responded that he had known all along, and that he needed to find out for sure about the inheritance. He was glad to report that the woman had both of them inside of her, especially Alice's beauty.

"Why are you here?" she asked, hoping his answer would be that he was only here for a visit and that he would leave immediately so that she could continue her nun duties.

"To give you another child," he said, without hesitation.

"I can't go through that again. I can't see another of my children raised by someone else," she said, tears flowing down her cheeks.

"You had your choice with our first daughter, and I honored your decision, but this time the option will be mine. Once you are pregnant, you will leave the Church and live a better life with me and our new child," he said, not changing his expression.

She cried. She explained that had he been around nineteen years ago, when the child had been born, that she might have changed her mind then and gone away with him.

"Are you ready to become pregnant?" he said his hands leaving her hair and caressing her arms.

She stared at him in disbelief at first. He had made his intention plain. He was here to get her pregnant again. But once their eyes met, she was caught up in his trance. She knew the decision was not hers. He would do what he wanted with her. God would not save her. Jesus would not save her. No one would save her.

"I am ready," she said, slipping out of her habit and letting it fall to the floor. The one good thing about the nun uniform was how easy it could be discarded.

He made love to her just as he had years ago. Sister Alice had only had sex with one person in her forty years, and that was twenty years ago. She hated him and loved him too. She knew her life would be centered around him now. As much as she hated to admit it, she was his property.

When the sex was over and he was fully clothed, he told her that a limo would be by to pick her up in the afternoon. She was not to ask questions; she was to get into the limo. He would see her later that evening.

Sister Alice knew she would get into the limo. She knew she would be with him again, and this time she was going to remain in his care. She hoped that she would be reunited with her daughter, but that hope might or might not come true. The Church had not saved her over the twenty-five years she had dedicated herself to Christ, and it would not save her now. She was now committed to Asmodais, even more committed to him than she was the Church. All through the time they had been apart, he had never left her thoughts. She had prayed for release from those images, but relief never came. She had devoted herself to the work of the Church in the hope that the Church would alter her visions and her love for Asmodais. The devotion had proven to be barely tolerable. The only thing that ever gave her hope was when she was with her daughter, the daughter Asmodais had given to her.

Asmodais called Angela Blanco. He wanted to visit some other women before spending the night at the compound. She picked him up outside of the nunnery and took him to another wealthy family in Darien. The man of the house was not at home, but the woman of the house and her teenage twin daughters supplied him with lunch and two hours of very good sex. He left all three quite pregnant and very ready to satisfy any other males they should encounter along the way.

While he waited for Angela to return, he communicated with Iblis and reported his current situation. He did not tell Iblis about Alice and her daughter; he had not mentioned them twenty years earlier. Iblis encouraged him to do more. His quota was still marginal at best. Lucifer was leading the converts with his false promises to the humans. Asmodais knew that Iblis detested Lucifer, but Lucifer was a good salesman and rarely missed his quotas.

Angela Blanco's limo pulled up beside him, and he entered the backseat of the limo. He smiled when he saw the two older women sitting beside Angela across from him.

"We have a short ride to the compound. I thought you might want a little snack," Angela said, smiling at him.

"Well, ladies. You're not teenagers. You're ripe and comely. Why, I bet you're still fertile," he asked, smiling across the seat at the two females, who appeared to be in their late thirties or early forties. He was using his jinn abilities to entrance them.

"I have had three children, and my friend has had two. We have not yet passed our childbearing years," one of the women reported.

He watched as both women undressed then slid across the space and joined him on his side of the limo. He asked Angela if she wanted to join them. Angela said "I'll watch. I like to watch too." He knew that she had very voyeuristic interests in his activities.

Winterhaven Security

As the limo entered the Winterhaven Security complex, Angela Blanco straightened her clothes then began to describe the features of the facility to Asmodais. The two women had been dropped off ten minutes earlier, and Angela had taken up sexually where they'd left off.

"We have a triple security network around the entire facility. There is an eighteen-foot wall made of slick stone, completely impossible to scale; on every inch of the wall, we have placed sensors that can detect anything as small as a fly touching the wall. A jolt of current is always going through the wall at all times. When we pull maintenance on the wall, it is done in sections, no two adjacent sections.

"The second security network is sensors on the ground throughout the compound. We have tested the sensors to make sure that they respond to a stimulus as small as a hamster running about on the ground. Again, no two adjacent sections are offline at the same time.

"The third security system is a microwave network that hides the facility from all air traffic involvement. We have verified that overhead satellites cannot penetrate the compound with their systems. We also verified with NASA and NSA that their satellites cannot penetrate the compound," she concluded.

"That is very good. You are on a par with the security network in France," Asmodais said calmly.

"You will soon discover that we have gone a few steps beyond the French compound in our internal security," she said, smiling at him.

"Explain."

"There is only a single point of entry to the compound through this road, which comes up into the underground parking garage on the third subbasement floor. From the second the automobile enters the first gate, until it reaches the parking garage, it undergoes rigid tests for contents such as bombs and any destructive material, both biological and chemical. If anything is detected that sets off an alarm, our staff have five seconds to turn off the alarm, or the vehicle will be detonated on the spot," she said.

"Can our staff react so quickly?" he asked.

"In the past they couldn't, but now, with the clone program operational for security measures, the clones can react very quickly and make very sane decisions. My husband will demonstrate the cloning for you shortly. Shall I continue?"

"Please do," he said smiling as his eyes scanned the scenic but deadly landscape.

"The main complex has two floors above ground and five floors below ground. Between each floor are concrete-reinforced floors five feet thick. There are no crawl spaces between the floors that lead to another floor in the building. I say that and that is not totally true. There are three elevator shafts. There's one that runs the entire seven floors, but it is only accessible for outside entry from the top floor, the garage entrance, and the computer room on the bottom floor. The second elevator shaft runs from the first floor to the fourth underground floor. This elevator is used by the security clones for their routine security checks. The third elevator runs from your office on the top floor to the computer room non-stop," she said.

"The clones are not allowed on the top floor and the bottom floor?" he asked.

"Yes, for another security measure. The main office, your office, is on the top floor, and we thought it inappropriate for clones to be bothering you at all hours of the day when there was no way for external people to get there from inside the building except coming through security measures. However, if they are required, they can be summoned to the main office. As far as the basement goes, we did a lot of research on that floor and did not think it appropriate to have the clones access this area for the same reasons," she said.

"The heliport?" he asked.

"The heliport can only be accessed through the top floor and through the main office, your office. It has a direct link to the mountain retreat for your own convenience. It can automatically travel the distance some twenty miles to the retreat in less than three minutes," she said, smiling.

"Sleeping quarters?" he asked.

"There are sleeping quarters on both the floors inhabited by humans, the top and the computer floor. The clones have a recharging room on the fourth subfloor. Your office is equipped for a six-month stay with no requirements from the outside world and heat-resistant furniture," she said.

"My staff?" he asked.

"You have a hand-picked staff of ten women at your disposal at anytime. They will be rotated when you are through with them or if they get pregnant. There will always be a fresh female staff member at your disposal. They are housed on the top floor in separate quarters. They do not leave the compound or the top floor until they are dismissed by you. They have been trained to serve you in any capacity that you desire. Their nationalities are truly global, and they are never in contact with each other. My husband is working on a clone of me that will replace and or enhance the current staff. Once my clone is completed, we will dismiss the others. Until the replacement occurs, you will find the current staff most delectable when you are ready to use them," she reported.

"And where will you be if I need you?" he asked.

"I have a desk in the corner of your office, but primarily I am based with my husband on the computer floor. I work with him on every project, but to answer your question, I carry a pager at all times so you can reach me when you need me. If you need me, press my number, and I will take the elevator from the computer floor to your office. I'll be there in no more than ten seconds. When I am not at the compound, I am usually at home with my husband, or I will be with you. We can both be here within ten minutes," she was assuring.

"And the retreat?" he asked.

"Nothing has changed in your retreat. Doctor Jane Wexler, your Paris-generated android, remains at the retreat doing research that you requested her to do many years ago. She does not keep me informed of the status of her research." She hated the fact there was something out of her control, but she dared not mention it.

"I have two people who will be joining me shortly to reside in the retreat. I will give you the details when they arrive."

"Yes, sir, we are entering the underground facility now," she reported.

"Does my current staff speak English?" he asked.

"Your staff is well-versed in several languages, plus the universal language of the body," she said as the limo came to a stop.

"Send a limo to the nunnery at Stamford and pick up Alice. I want her brought to me within the hour. See to it that there is a fire and that another nun's body is found in the fire. I want no one to know of Sister Alice's disappearance for a while," he ordered.

"Should I go with the limo or should I go with you to your quarters?" She wanted to be with him but it was his decision.

"Take me to my quarters," he ordered.

Deacon Marsala Finds out too Late

Deacon Domenico Marsala looked at the young boy who was resting peacefully on the bed in St. Joe's Hospital. Today, after noon Mass, he had seen the boy go downstairs to change. He knew the boy was changing to return to the bishop, but obviously Asmodais had gotten to him first. He did not approve of the way the bishop handled the young altar boys throughout the state. This was child molestation at its worst, and this had been brought up at the VEF meeting. The VEF were not to interfere with the bishops. The Church Council would clean up their own bishops and priests. The rules had been established, and whether he liked the rules or not, they were the rules. This was the bishop's territory, and he was not here to judge the bishop. He was here for one primary reason—to assassinate Asmodais Winters.

Had Asmodais been at the Mass? Had he known about the relationship between the bishop and the young altar boy? Was this attack meant to warn the bishop, or was it intended to warn him and the Vatican Elite Force that Asmodais was in charge of his own destiny? Asmodais had been here twenty years earlier. Had he corrupted this parish beyond help? This was something Marsala would have to discover and report when the mission was completed.

He stared at the boy. The comatose condition had ended. The boy was still heavily sedated. Was that a smile on the boy's face? If he was sedated, then how could he have discernable facial features? Was the boy simply resting after the ordeal? Had Asmodais destroyed the future of this young man too? What would happen once the boy returned to normal? What was *normal*? Would anyone who had sex with this boy in the future be subject to the whims of Asmodais?

Unfortunately, to all these questions, there was only one answer. The boy had been abused by Asmodais; his life would never again be his own life unless he could be saved. The spreading of holy water and holy oil on the body of the boy had proven ineffective. Asmodais had gone out of his way to destroy this young male. Marsala had to make a quick decision if he wanted to save the boy at all. He could not allow the boy to corrupt other people. This order came directly from the Vatican Elite Force Command—any person attacked by evil who could not be saved should be eliminated. He reached into his vest pocket. He extracted the holy water and a syringe. He filled the needle with holy water and shot in directly into the IV tube bringing fluids to the boy. The boy would either die from the dosage, or he would live. Marsala prayed for the boy to survive. The life would be determined by how much Asmodais had destroyed the body from inside. He left the hospital room when a nurse came into the room.

He was in the cafeteria some ten minutes later when he heard the news of the death of the boy. He was disappointed when the introduction of holy water directly into the bloodstream had been unable to save the boy. Marsala closed his eyes briefly and prayed for the boy's soul.

Marsala drove back to the rectory. He had to figure out why Asmodais would venture out on Easter morning and go to Mass in public. Asmodais must know that he was a doomed man if spotted in public by a VEF agent, but he had been to this church for a reason. Thus far, there were no signs that Asmodais was worried about anything. Marsala had to learn why Asmodais Winters was so secure in his safety. He had been secure enough to visit the attendant. He had been secure enough to delay his departure with the woman in 301. He had been secure enough to attend Mass. He had been secure enough to attack the altar boy. Marsala had to determine what that reasons were. Perhaps if he knew why Asmodais had been there, then he might be able to plan his next move.

He spoke first to the senior priest and asked him if there was something special about the service for that day. The priest said only that it had been Easter Sunday, and a lot more people attend Mass on Easter than any other day, with the exception of Christmas.

He then went to speak with Mother Superior, who appeared to be in a frightfully sad mood.

"What is the matter?" he asked her.

"The Church just lost one of its most devoted nuns, Sister Alice. She has been with us for twenty-five years, and now she is gone," Mother Superior said with tears flowing down her cheeks.

"What do you mean, *gone*? Did she die?" Marsala asked.

"Yes, there was a fire in her cell an hour ago. When the firemen finished their work, we found the remains," Mother Superior responded.

"Tell me more about this nun," he said.

"There is not much to tell. Sister Alice came to the nunnery out of the Catholic orphanage in Hartford when she was eighteen. She was young, but she was very dedicated. She did have a problem with her faith about twenty years ago, but she got over the issue and has been a stalwart in the community since then. She was loved by everyone," the Mother Superior said, wiping away her tears with a small white handkerchief.

"Tell me about this problem with her faith. Could it have something to do with a man?" he asked.

"I don't know. I wasn't the Mother Superior at that time, but I do recall hearing the previous Mother Superior saying how proud she was of Sister Alice for continuing her life in the Church when she could have just as easily gone another direction. The records could have told you more, but the records of twenty years ago were burned in a fire around a year later. We had not begun the process of microfilming the records at that time," Mother Superior said.

"Could Sister Alice have conceived a child?" Deacon Marsala asked.

"I really can't say. I don't see how that is possible, but I really don't know. The one thing I know is that Sister Alice was very good and very tolerant with the young people of the parish," Mother Superior said.

"Anyone she cared for more than the others?" he asked.

"Not that I can recall. Sister Alice and I were as close as anyone, I guess. We took our vows at the same time. But I can't recall her being especially close to any one child," Mother Superior said.

"Thanks for your time. Is there any other nun who had a close friendship or a particular relationship with Sister Alice?" he asked. He knew that close friendships or "particular relationships," as they are called, are not encouraged in religious communities. Impartial Christian fellowship is the goal.

"She was well liked by everyone. I can't think of anyone in particular," Mother Superior said, as she backed away. She wasn't about to tell this man how really close she and Sister Alice had been over the years.

Deacon Marsala stared at the woman as she left. Too many things were not adding up to him. Sister Alice had an issue with the Church twenty years ago. Asmodais had been here twenty years ago. Could it be that Asmodais got a nun pregnant? Why would Asmodais do such an evil thing? Demons and jinns were not allowed to touch the saintly.

That answer was simple. He was Asmodais. He would dare anything. Asmodais had returned to the church for Mass today.

He knew Asmodais had been with the altar boy. Had he also been with Sister Alice again? Why would he be with her again? She was twenty years older than she had been when he had been here the first time. How much had Sister Alice aged? If she had become pregnant, then what happened to the child? Was the child a boy or a girl? He thought the answer to that question was easy. The child had to be a girl. There was no way Asmodais would have left his son to be raised by others for nineteen years. Besides, in his study of demons, the word was that Iblis could only produce "half-jinn" sons, and Asmodais could only produce half-jinn daughters from humans. So where was the child? The church records were burned, but there had to be some trace of the girl. How many other children had Asmodais left here on his last visit? Was he here to start another population explosion in nine months? How corrupt was this community?

He wasn't going to get any answers at the church. He needed to go do some local research at the public library. If this child was out there, and if she had a direct link with Asmodais, then he needed to find her quickly. If Asmodais had killed Sister Alice, what would be his next move?

Asmodais had not killed Sister Alice! There is no way that he would return to America and take the chance of getting caught just to murder the mother of his child. This was not something Asmodais would do. It didn't fit his profile. What did fit Asmodais's profile was an effort to bring the wayward nun back into his family. He didn't know who died in that fire last night, but he was certain it wasn't Sister Alice. He would get Mother Superior to check the absence of other nuns later.

Asmodais Strikes First

Asmodais Winters heard of the death of the stewardess and the altar boy from research performed by Angela Blanco on her laptop. He was more than irate about the deaths of these two converts. Iblis would be just as upset if his quota was not met. The last thing he needed was Iblis upset with him. He called Angela Blanco into the office from the computer room. She was there within ten seconds. He slapped her so hard that she fell to the carpeted floor. She bounced up immediately and was ready if he needed to inflict punishment on her again. He told her of the death of the stewardess and the altar boy without slapping her a second time.

Angela asked what steps he wanted to take with the VEF agent. His response was simple. He wanted the man to be killed immediately. He didn't care what resources it took to complete the assignment; he wanted it done before the day was over.

Angela made one quick call on her cell phone and told him she had hired a hit team to take care of the agent. She had given the assignment to a team of men that had never failed her in the past. She felt confident the job would be done quickly and expeditiously.

That was not enough to satisfy Asmodais. He wanted her to supervise the deaths personally. She said that she would leave immediately and join the men.

He told her he needed replacements for the two servants who had been killed by Marsala, and he needed them today. She made another quick call, and once she hung up she told him that a young woman and a young man would be at the compound within thirty minutes to replace the two who had died at the hands of the VEF agent.

He waited for her to leave before he called one of the female staff into the office. She was a tall woman who appeared to be of German descent. She had to be at least six foot tall which put her almost at eye level with him. Her body had strong features that any German man would appreciate. She was a true platinum blonde, fair-skinned and blue-eyed and strong-boned.

He slapped her when she was close enough to be slapped. She fell backward but did not fall to the floor. After a brief second, she stood erect. He could see the pain and humiliation on her face. It excited him. She had been trained well by Angela and her team.

He grabbed her by the arm and forced her into the bedroom attached to the office. The room was barren except for the huge bed against one wall. The room was pitch-black, with no windows and no apparent lighting. He did not need light to see in the dark. In fact, he preferred the darkness.

He ripped off her clothes then literally tossed her onto the bed. Moments later, he was inside the female. Unfortunately, because of his anger at the agent, he forgot the woman was not a clone or an android. The heat from his body melted her, and her remains were burned to a crisp that would be unidentifiable by even the best medical examiner. He tossed her aside, then called in another staff member and took more care to not roast her as he made her pregnant.

Angela Blanco met the two men a block from the Winterhaven Complex. She leaped into the back of their van, and the trio sped away.

She told the men that this mission was critical, and it must be done immediately. One of the men climbed into the back of the van with her. She knew what he wanted to do with her. It would not be the first time she had shared her body with the two assassins. They had proven themselves reliable twice before when it was necessary. She told the man who joined her that as soon as Marsala was dead, she would give him everything he wanted from her, including her body. The two men had been rewarded in past assassinations with sex and money from her.

The one who had joined her was not interested in the future. He wanted a piece of her before the mission. He slapped her and had his way with her while the van sped toward the rectory. She knew better than to fight him. He was larger and more vicious than most men she knew—that was why she hired him. She allowed him to rape her.

When they arrived at the rectory, she spotted the Malibu that had been given to Marsala the day before. She had seen the car in the parking lot of the complex where the stewardess had lived and at the rectory on Easter morning. She pointed it out to the men. Marsala was obviously still at the rectory.

She watched from the front seat of the van as the men planted an explosive outside the automobile and beneath the driver's side seat. From the amount of explosive the men used, she knew it was overkill, but this mission was critical. Could there really be *overkill?* She was certain Asmodais would not think so.

Now it was a waiting game until the agent returned to his vehicle. While they were waiting, the second man decided it was his time to get his early reward in the back of the van. Angela let him enjoy her body while the other man sat in the front seat and kept watch for the victim. Once the man in the backseat had finished with her, she was asked to leave the van and wait elsewhere. She told them that Asmodais had told her to remain and supervise the entire execution. They explained that they worked alone. She could watch from a safe distance, but she could not remain with them.

She left the van and walked into a diner across the street from the rectory. She took a window seat where she could observe the van and the vehicle. She could only wait for the action to take place.

Marsala saw the woman enter the diner and quickly hid in a booth before she noticed him. He had seen her get out of the van and come to the diner. Had the men dismissed her? He observed that she was watching the van and his car intently. From his vantage point, he noted the two men in the van, both smoking cigarettes and staring at his car. Obviously Asmodais had put out a hit on him. This woman was part of the hit team, but why was she here? Why wasn't she with the men in the van? Were they so sure of themselves that they didn't want her around to take the credit for the kill?

He eased out of the booth and made it to the back exit of the diner without her seeing him leave. He crossed the street behind the van, hoping the men would be so focused on their target that they wouldn't notice him. He knew he had to act quickly because the woman would be able to see him if she looked hard enough toward the back of the van.

Marsala knelt and spotted the package beneath the front side of his car. They had planted a bomb to blow him up. Too bad they had not planted the device and driven away. They might have succeeded in killing him had they not made such a simple mistake. But such is the vanity of hired killers. Marsala pulled out his German Luger, his favorite weapon, and aimed it at the package beneath his car. The water silencer on his Luger barely made a sound thanks to a train going by the area, but the noise of the explosion of his car shook the area.

The confusion gave him the additional seconds he needed to run to the open driver's side window of the van and shoot the two men in the front seat immediately. He spotted more of the explosive material in the back of the van and took a burning cigarette from the driver's dead lips and tossed the cigarette toward the material. He streaked away from the van and into the rectory before anyone could notice him. He hid in the shrubbery and awaited the second explosion.

He watched as the woman exited the diner and headed toward the van. She was still twenty feet from the van when the second explosion went off. She was knocked off her feet and landed on her butt at the entrance to the restaurant. He felt like shooting her from his hiding place, but too many people were in the open area and in his line of fire.

He watched as she made a telephone call with her cell phone. He remained hidden and watched as she pulled away in a limo. The limo had the WH on the side and *Winterhaven* etched in big letters. He waited for the limo to disappear completely before he emerged from his hiding place.

Angela Blanco was satisfied with the results of the execution. While she had not seen the agent actually enter the vehicle, it had exploded. She had wondered why the van had exploded, but she knew the men had been smoking. Perhaps the blast of the explosion had shaken the van, and one of the lit cigarettes had fallen into the back of the van. She was just lucky that she had not reentered the van before it blew up. In fact, if she had been a few feet closer, she would not have escaped death at all.

She was also happy that she had saved the expense of paying the hit men off. Sure they had gotten a reward with sex from her, but no money had been spent. She would tell Asmodais she had paid them off and collect the money for herself.

She went directly to the Winterhaven compound and to the main office, where she smiled when she saw Asmodais and the two replacements having a drink. From the smiles on faces, she knew that Asmodais was finished with them. She called a guard and had the two people escorted out of the complex.

Asmodais asked, once they were alone, if the agent was dead. She told him what had happened, and he seemed pleased with her results. He rewarded her devotion in the back of his office. He told her that Sister Alice was in one of the back bedrooms and was not to be disturbed tonight.

Later Angela took him to visit another family in New Canaan, where they both spent the night with four women and two men.

She took care of the men while he impregnated the women. He said he was still off quota, but now that the VEF agent had been disposed of, he could work more freely for a few days. He had no doubts that the VEF would be sending someone to replace Marsala, but by the time the new agents reached America and traced Marsala's steps, he would be out of America and back in Paris.

Early the next morning, she headed back to the compound, and he drove a red Porsche away for personal business.

Jenny Lynn Finds Her Parents

It was early Monday morning; Jenny Lynn was riding Smoke, her favorite stallion, when she saw the red Porsche convertible enter the long driveway to the Lynn estate. She recognized the man wearing the dark sunglasses from a long distance. He was the man that had visited her in her dreams so many times in the past. It was his face that she would go to sleep with at night, and he would be the last thing she remembered in her dreams. She recognized him as the man who had stood beside her in the back of the church the day before. She had allowed him to mentally fondle her while the bishop gave his speech. Then she'd gone downstairs with him. She had freely given her most prized possession to him, her virginity, on the table in that small classroom. She had never expected to see the man again, but here he was. He had found her. She had to know why he was there. Was he there to take possession of her? She definitely hoped so.

She punched the stallion gently with her toe, and the stallion lurched forward like he had done so many times in the past. Riding him now made her think of the way the man had rode her yesterday. They both were so strong, and she felt she could control both of them. God, she loved being in control of such power. She guided him past the snow that remained on the ground. She knew the estate very well. She made it to the corral almost the same time the Porsche came to a stop in the front yard. She considered running to the man, but her adopted father, Jerry Lynn, had always told her, "Take care of your animals first then tend to the world."

She knew that Jerry and Michele Lynn were not her real parents. They had told her that they had adopted her when she was very small. They never told her who her real parents were, but she was sure they knew. She dreamed of her parents. She dreamed the man at Mass yesterday was her father. She dreamed he would be the father of her child too.

She walked Smoke to the stall and brushed him down. He needed to be taken care of before she could return to the house. She could not rush the job and expect Smoke to have respect for her.

Asmodais Winters was met at the door by Michele Lynn, who had a confused smile when she opened the door. He had not seen her in a few years, since her last visit to Paris. Michele Lynn was attractive, but not overly so. She had short dark hair; life on a horse farm had kept her fit and shapely. She was a bit of a lush and often had found a willing partner to bring her home from parties. Her husband Jerry Lynn was not a party animal at all. He was into investments and making money on Wall Street. He worked long hours, and Asmodais thought that might be the reason that Michele drank so much and was always looking for partners to fulfill her basic needs. Jerry Lynn also had a very available and sexy secretary.

The smile on Michele's face when she opened the front door told him that she was confused but available if he wanted her. Jerry was obviously not at home. He had met her before in Paris when she was on vacation, so she knew exactly who he was and why he was here.

"She's in the barn taking care of her stallion. She'll join us in twenty minutes or so," the dark-haired woman said as she stepped back from the door and allowed him to enter.

"Where is Jerry?" he asked, waiting as she closed the door and joined him.

"He had to go to town for a business meeting. I expect him back before lunch. How long can you stay?" responding and providing a tantalizing smile for him to see.

"Long enough to pick up my daughter and perhaps tend to some extra business while I am waiting," following her into the large den area.

The room was spacious and ornate with expensive paintings and books. A wet bar was at one end of the room. He noticed a half-empty pitcher of Bloody Marys and a half-empty glass. She obviously had been drinking this morning while her daughter was riding. She walked to the bar but did not pour herself a fresh drink or offer him one. She was attempting to prove to him that she was a good mother to Jenny.

"I hope I am part of the extra business, Master," she said, turning slowly to face him and allowing her short skirt to float away from her thigh, exposing her shapely legs. The morning sunlight came through the glass door behind her and seemed to flow through the short skirt. The light made it seem as if she was undressed.

"You look as fresh as you did three years ago when I last saw you in Paris. You and Jerry have done a wonderful job raising my daughter," moving to her and cupping her face in his hands.

"We have always been proud to serve you, Master," she said, batting her eyes at him.

He pulled her face close to his and kissed her, filling her mouth with his tongue. She was eagerly receptive to his lips and tongue. He recalled how much she had enjoyed this type of foreplay. Some women preferred to be fondled before their weaknesses could be exploited, but not Michele Lynn. One of her major weaknesses with males in general had always been kissing. Once a man or even a teenage boy pressed his lips against her lips, even if he was only halfway decent at the action, he would find the rest of his goals readily attainable.

Her body almost fused with his body, and their clothes seemed inconsequential. Her need for sexual relief was paramount. She was prepared to give everything to him. When the moment was completed, she led him upstairs and to the master bedroom. She removed her clothes on the stairs leading to the room. She was ready to serve him as soon as the door was closed. He took his time with her as he had three years earlier.

"Thank you, Master, I have needed that for a very long time," she said as they both dressed after the sex was over.

"I will need some time alone with my daughter. Pack her a few things. I am sure she will be leaving with me today."

"Yes, Master," she responded and quickly left the room. She had much more spring in her step than she had before they had sex.

He walked downstairs and found the beautiful red-haired young woman in the drawing room waiting for him. She had changed out of her riding gear and was sporting a short skirt and a stunning blouse. He wondered when she had changed. Had she stopped by her room while he was with her adopted mother? Had she overheard the sex between the two adults? She was standing near the trophy wall where all of her equestrian trophies were displayed. She obviously wanted him to notice her accomplishments. She turned toward him and smiled. She had a figure just like her mother, Sister Alice, and an enticing way of carrying herself.

She hesitated a few seconds, as she tried for exactly the right greeting to give him. He was about to say something to her but she was quicker: "Hello, Father."

"You know?" Had she figured this out on her own, or had Jerry or Michele Lynn already explained him to her?

"I have dreamed of you since I was five years old. I dreamed of what my father would look like, and a vision of you always appeared. I dreamed that you would come to me, would want me and that I would give myself to you. Yesterday, I knew it at the church. That is the reason I moved to where you were standing in the back. I consider myself a true judge of character when it comes to people, but when you mentally enjoyed me, I knew I was in a league above me. There is only one person on the face of the Earth who could have done what you did to me. That person had to be someone much stronger than I am. Now, since I have rarely met a man stronger than I am, the only conclusion I could draw was that you were my father." She was proud of her logical powers of observation.

"Do you know who your mother is?" he asked, stopping near her.

"Yes, I think so. Again, logically, the woman would have to be a very strong person and would have to be around all the time as I was growing up. The person would have to be a person I could confide in and trust to always come up with the decision that would be best for me. Not necessarily the choices I would think were best for me, but the best options for me in the long range. I trusted her over the years, and I believe she loved me even more for earning the trust from afar. I am sure my adopted parents know who she is, but they have never mentioned her name. It is Sister Alice," she said looking for agreement from him.

"You are a very intelligent child and speak better than children your age," he said, grasping her hands in his larger hands.

"I get that from both of you. Now the real question is … why you are here?" Jenny looked Asmodais in the eyes.

He could sense that she wasn't afraid of him. Most females, even half-jinn females, cowered before him and obeyed him without question, but this young woman definitely had a mind of her own. Was that because of his seed, or was that something she inherited from her mother? He hoped it was from his seed.

"I am here to bring my favorite American family back together," stroking her hand.

"Why? So that you can leave us again?" she said in a sarcastic tone.

"Ah, you do have your mother's sarcasm," he laughed. "But that is not my intention at all. I wish us to be together for a very long time."

"And where do I fit into this family picture?" she asked.

"Where to you want to fit?" he asked.

"I like the role of daughter, but I think I am more suited for another role," she said in an arrogant voice.

"And what role do you think you are qualified to fill?" he asked her.

"Yesterday you gave me a sample of what sex would be like with you. I didn't do what you told me to do. I did have sex with my boyfriend last night for the first time. He really enjoyed the sex. Trust me, he wasn't half as satisfying as you, and you didn't even try that hard. I have the body that you and my mother gave me. I have the intelligence you both gave me. I have your arrogance and the patience of my mother. I now want more, a lot more. I want it all," she said, without smiling.

"And what do you think *it all* is?" he asked, wondering where this conversation was headed.

"I want to bear you a son. I have dreamed my entire life so far of how I would produce you a son. I want to do it," she said, looking up at him.

He frowned. "I don't know if that is possible."

"Listen, you didn't come back here after twenty years to claim me unless I had something that you thought was very important. You did not check me out at the church, take my virginity, then return to me today simply because I was a good fuck at church. Now whatever your plan is for me, let's get on with it," she argued.

"Are you ready to go?" he asked as he saw Michele Lynn coming down the stairs with a bag.

Michele Lynn entered the room carrying the suitcase and wearing a very contented smile on her face.

"Thanks, Michele, I hope my father's child inside you brings you comfort," Jenny laughed as she took the bag and flew out the front door.

"I have a child inside me?" Michele asked, beaming as she stared at Asmodais.

"Yes," he responded then turned and left her. He doubted he would ever see her again, but that would be no major loss to him. She had been available, and that was all there was to it. She had merely been another quota item for Iblis.

Jenny was already sitting in the red convertible Porsche when he reached the car. He didn't see where she had stashed her luggage, but he had seen her leave the church in a Porsche with the young man, so she probably knew the interior of the car better than he did.

"Can I get a car like this one?" she asked as he got behind the steering wheel.

"You can have any vehicle your heart desires," he assured her as he started the car.

"I don't really care about the car … you know what I really want," she said, caressing his right leg.

He drove away from the Lynn estate.

The drive to the Winterhaven compound took thirty-five minutes, but soon the two of them were upstairs on the second floor in Asmodais's office. Waiting for them was Sister Alice, no longer wearing the habit. She was dressed in a stunning blue suit that accentuated her still-girlish figure and her flowing red hair.

"Mom, you look outstanding," Jenny Lynn said, approaching her mother.

"You know?" Alice asked as they hugged. She gave Asmodais a questioning glance.

"I figured out you were my real mother many months ago, but I didn't know how to approach you," Jenny said, squeezing her mother tightly and answering the question before her father could respond.

"Thank you, Asmodais, for finally making us a family again," Alice said to Asmodais. "You don't know how often I have prayed for this moment."

"No problem, but we need to leave," Asmodais said as he led them toward the heliport.

"Are we going somewhere?" Alice asked as the hugging ended.

"Mom, he has a reason for wanting us to leave. Let's not argue," Jenny said as she held onto her mother's hand.

"She is headstrong just like you," Asmodais laughed. "Angela, we will be using the heliport. Is it ready?"

"Yes, sir, it is ready," Angela Blanco responded from her desk in the corner of the office.

Marsala Gains Support

Marsala poured over the records in the public library, devouring articles published over the past twenty years. He read the reports of the fires at the nunnery and the death of the Mother Superior a year later. There had been two new Mother Superiors over the past fifteen years. Asmodais had covered his tracks very well, but no one could be that good, especially when he was no longer in America. Someone had to make a mistake somewhere. Asmodais would not have made the mistake if he had been present, but his trust of people could only lead to mistakes.

He traced adoptions in that period of time, especially for little girls. There were three adoptions, but there was paperwork on all three. So he decided the adoption was not entirely legal. He did notice a high rate of childbirths about a year after Asmodais would have been in America. Could Asmodais have been that prolific while he had been in America? Marsala's goal was identifying the child of Sister Alice. He didn't have time to focus on all the other possibilities. Asmodais would expect him to go off onto tangents. He had to remain focused.

It wasn't until he started reviewing the sports events five years later that a name seemed to come out of nowhere. A young girl who had recently turned four had won an equestrian Pony Club event. She was young at four, but since her parents backed her, then her age was accepted. She was a local girl. She was the daughter of Jerry and Michele Lynn. He had seen the parents' names before, so he did a quick marriage search. The two had been married almost twenty years ago, more like nineteen years than twenty. Jerry had just hit it big in the stock market, which was strange because he was a neophyte in the trading business. It happens, but not that often. The pictures of their wedding showed a very slim and beautiful dark-haired young woman. At another gala party six months, later she was shown with a small baby at a christening. There had been no pictures of Michele Lynn or any reports of her pregnancy for the six months between the two photos. Both the parents were dark-haired, and yet the daughter had red, almost flaming, hair. They had told reporters that the red hair came from some great-uncle or something and was not that unusual. Something told Marsala that this child had to be the missing child of Sister Alice. It could be confirmed if Sister Alice had red hair. Of course, that fact would be hard to prove without the physical body of Sister Alice.

He continued to search for stories about the Lynn child through the papers and school work. She had attended Catholic school and had excelled in almost everything. In most of Jenny Lynn's school pictures, Sister Alice was in the background. Sister Alice was obviously watching over her child.

He closed the pages. Now he was convinced that Jenny Lynn was the daughter of Asmodais and Sister Alice. What was his next step?

Samantha Lee stared across the library at the man skimming local news stories. The man appeared to be in his late fifties and had a regal appearance. She knew who he was. She had seen him at Mass on Sunday when the bishop mentioned his name. She had gone back to her apartment after Mass and researched his name in the FBI files. His name was Deacon Domenico Marsala, and he worked directly for Interpol and the Vatican Elite Force. According to the dictates of the FBI, this man was off-limits to everyone. He was not to be hampered or deterred in performing his assignment. If he requested assistance, then agents were to provide him with anything he needed within reason.

Samantha was an FBI agent and had worked for the FBI more years than she cared to admit. She was dedicated to solving crimes and had a good record in that endeavor. She had been responsible for bringing over thirty criminals to justice. She liked working for the FBI, but she knew she was destined to do more than merely be a servant to the FBI. She wondered if Deacon Domenico Marsala was her avenue to her new destiny or the fulfillment of the destiny she hoped for. She had been on her Director's Bad list for months. He had told her that he did not approve of all her processes and procedures. Of course he approved of her results. They all do.

His research had brought him to Jerry Lynn. She knew Jerry Lynn like the back of her hand. She had followed his career for the past ten years and observed from the sidelines how wealthy the man had become. Jerry Lynn had started in the investment business with a tip on Winterhaven Security when the company had started in America. It had been a real gamble, but a successful one. The FBI had often speculated that Jerry Lynn was getting insider information but had yet to prove any connection to wrongdoing.

Possibly with the support of the VEF agent, the FBI investigation could be completed successfully, and she would be moved from her current assignment to one more investigative and more to her liking. Although she was very good locally and had used locals to help her, she really wanted more national and global interaction.

"Winterhaven," Samantha Lee called out as she approached the man at the table.

Marsala turned and smiled as a young female sat down next to him at the table. Pleasing to his eye, she appeared to be in her late twenties, with short blonde hair and a nice tan.

"Winterhaven?" The name rang a bell. It had been the name etched on the limo that had picked up the woman from the diner.

"You were about to ask yourself how Jerry Lynn made all his money in such a very short period of time on the stock market, weren't you? Hi, my name is Samantha Lee. I work for the FBI. Please do not call me Sam. I hate that name," she said.

"Hi, I am Deacon Domenico Marsala," he said, smiling at her.

"Just my luck, isn't it? I find a good-looking man with no wedding ring on his finger, and he has to be a priest," she laughed.

"I am associated with Interpol and the Vatican. Trust me, though, *Deacon* is purely an honorific title. I went through that phase in my life, and I am now about as far removed from the priesthood as a person can be," he said, smiling at her.

"Are you celibate?" she asked.

"Not in the least. I appreciate women on many levels, including the sexual," he responded.

Samantha liked that response. She was happy he wasn't one of those pious people who frown on sex. Hopefully he wasn't going to be like her director who hated it when she used sex to get what he she wanted. She liked sex. She wondered how sex would be with him.

Marsala thought this was strange. This woman was boldly forward. He had just met her, and she was asking him questions like they were at a bar somewhere. But he found that he did like her. She did have a certain appeal, and not all of it was sexual.

"Good! Now that we have the introductions over with, let's get to some facts about the Winterhaven topic," she said, running her fingers through some of the paper on the table.

"You seem to be the one doing the talking, so please continue."

"Winterhaven, as far as anyone knows, is a French company specializing in security and other services. We, in the FBI, have been looking at them closely for twenty years, ever since they popped up on the radar. They have a single owner, Asmodais Winters, and as far as we know, he has been around for more than fifty years, running branches of the company in seven major countries, including Britain, Russia, and China. He was in China when Nixon opened the trading doors to that country. He has never once been caught on camera by anyone. One would think a man as powerful as Asmodais Winters would enjoy being photographed all the time," she said.

"Interesting," Marsala said, "what does this have to do with Jerry Lynn?"

"Jerry Lynn was the first trader to jump on the Winterhaven bandwagon when the stock was less than ten cents a share. In six months, the stocks were taken off the table—but not before he became a multimillionaire. After the initial investment, he has only invested in stocks that have made him a fortune. No one in the trading business can be that lucky," she said.

"We should perhaps make a visit to Winterhaven," he said wondering if this was what she was suggesting.

"That is easier said than done. That place is tighter than Fort Knox or even Vatican City," she said, staring down at a photo of the outside of the Winterhaven complex.

"But the FBI can get in there, can't they?"

"Sure, for a scheduled visit, but I doubt we'd see anything they don't want us to see," she said, forcing a smile.

"Then schedule it. I want to see this place. I also want to visit this Jenny Lynn girl," he ordered, slightly raising his voice. He knew it might be bold for him to start giving her orders, but he really didn't have time to play her silly games. Either she was going to help him, or she wasn't. He needed to know her commitment as quickly as possible. If she wasn't going to help him, then he would have to make plans of his own.

"I doubt that she is home. I watched the house early this morning, and I saw her leave with an overnight bag with a man in a red convertible Porsche," not flinching from the obvious orders he had given her.

"Did you get any pictures of the man she left with?" he asked.

"I got some photos with a zoom lens, but I was too far away. I reviewed them. He is more of a blur. I am going to have to check my camera when I get back to headquarters," she reported.

"Don't bother, there is probably nothing wrong with your camera. Asmodais probably has a filter over the entire estate to maintain security. I believe he is the father of the girl," he said.

She gave him a funny look. He guessed that the thought had not crossed her mind. He doubted she had many clues as to why Asmodais was in America.

"You want to go get something to eat?" She changed the subject.

"Sure, I am staying at the rectory. I can vouch that the food is barely edible there!" Marsala laughed.

"Then we can go to my place. I have tons of food that I will never be able to eat alone." Samantha rose from her chair.

"Won't your partner or boyfriend be jealous when you bring home a strange man?"

"My partner is working another case in Washington, and I ditched my freeloading bum of a boyfriend a month ago. He thought he was God's gift to women. Trust me, I know better," she said, giving him a big teasing smile.

Marsala decided not to fight her. She was offering free food and possibly some help on the case. Perhaps God had sent her to give him some assistance. It wouldn't have been the first time he had accepted help from the weaker sex, if you could call women the weaker sex.

"My car or yours?" he asked rising too. The senior priest had supplied him a new car after his car had exploded at the rectory.

"We can walk from here. I only live about four blocks from the library. This is my second office." She led him toward the side door of the building. The sign on the door read NO EXIT, but that didn't stop her from walking right through the door. No bells or alarms went off. She had obviously been through the door many times in the past.

"Let me stop by my car and at least get us a bottle of wine for dinner," he said as the two of them left the library together.

The Retreat

"Wow! That was a sensational ride," Jenny Lynn said as the three on them exited from the helicopter.

"Where are we?" Alice glanced around nervously.

"In my special place that only few people have ever seen or will ever see. This place was created over fifty years ago and has been kept a complete secret. There is only one way into the retreat and only one way out. The cliffs are like glass, making certain no one can climb the cliffs, and even if they did, there are other safety measures. Make yourself at home and familiarize yourself with everything. I have to go see the only person here," he said.

The main room of the cave was the largest of all the rooms. The sides were all paneled in mahogany. The ceiling was carved from stone and had a shellac finish. From the main room to the front was the heliport area, which was enclosed once the helicopter was in place. A one-way see-through wall was beyond the heliport that overlooked the valley below. To the left of the main room was a large kitchen area that also supported an eating room. To the left of the kitchen entrance was a small hallway that led to three bedrooms. Each bedroom had an accompanying full bathroom. One of the bedrooms had a view of a waterfall beyond it. The streaming water hid the windowed view. To the right of the main room were two doors. One of the doors led to an office area with computers and four enormous bookcases. The other door led to a hallway that disappeared into the bowels of the cave.

"Dad," Jenny called to him.

He turned to her as she approached him. Rarely had anyone ever called him that name.

"Thanks for finally getting us all together again!" She gave him a hug.

"No problem, honey," he said then disappeared.

He moved toward the second door on the right, then down a dark passageway, hitting several concealed buttons along the way. If he had forgotten those buttons, the walls would have sprayed a deadly gas. The gas would not kill him, but it would kill snooping humans. He turned off the hallway and descended a set of stairs. Only the hand rail on the side kept a person from falling into a vast cavern. Near the bottom he pressed another button, and the wall opened. He stepped inside, and the room automatically became bright. He spotted the single chair in the middle of the room.

The chair was large and similar to a dentist's or gynecologist's chair without all the attached hardware. A dentist or a female doctor who wanted to enjoy the patients would have loved a chair like this.

"It is ready," a female voice called from behind a dark glass panel at the far end of the cave.

He waited for her to appear. Immediately a drop-dead gorgeous, dark-haired woman in a body suit that accentuated all her features came into view.

"Hello, Jane, it is good to see you again. I think you get more gorgeous every time I see you," he said, approaching her.

"Thank you, sir. I am what you made me," Jane said as she approached.

She was right; he had physically made her many years ago. She was a fully functional robot with a human form. Angela Blanco's husband had built clones, but those clones were nowhere as perfect as his Jane Wexler android.

"I need to release energy," he said, moving toward the empty chair.

She undressed then eased down into the chair. "My body is ready, sir." She gave him a robotic smile.

He took off his clothes. The lights in the room automatically shut off. The pitch blackness of the room was eerie; it was even darker than his bedroom at the office. He went to the chair and mounted the android. Immediately his body began to glow, and seconds later her body began to glow too. He entered her, and as the sex unfurled she became the receptacle that no human woman could ever become. The room became a bright light, brilliant enough to blind a human even if she did not look directly into it.

Forty-five minutes later, the explosion he needed happened, and his juices flowed into the womanlike body. The brightness faded, and the other lights came back on automatically as he regained his human form.

She arose silently and went behind the wall. He followed her. She stepped into a small glassed-in room. He watched as she cleaned the fluid from inside her womb and placed the fluid in a very dark flask. She sealed the flask and placed it into an incubator.

"How long will it survive?" he asked.

"Twenty hours."

"Run your test on it. Twenty hours is good, but for it to survive, it must be inside a woman for twenty-four hours and not lose potency during that period of time. Do you have enough?"

"Yes, sir, I will ship some to Paris for my counterpart to test too," she said.

"Good."

"You do know, sir, that the time could be greatly reduced if this was placed directly into a woman's womb from you," she said.

"Yes, Jane, I know that. We have tried that many times over the years, but the woman always dies during the intercourse period. The heat is too high for the fragile female body," he said.

"I will succeed this time," she said. "My goal is thirty hours."

Asmodais left the android and returned to the two women in the main area. He found Jenny alone.

"Mother tells me that she is pregnant again," Jenny said, smiling at him.

"Yes, she will have another daughter in nine months."

"Is there a chance that she will have a son?"

"No, it will be a daughter just like I gave Michele Lynn," he said.

"I want your son." Jenny moved toward him.

"I know, and I am working on it. It is not as easy to sire a son as a daughter."

"It is because a female body is too fragile, right?"

"Yes, something like that."

"I thought so. The fact that I am the daughter of a godly person and Asmodais, Prince of Lust, a demon, doesn't help, does it?"

"I wish it was that simple. I have attempted to produce male offspring from many saintly women, but the result is always the same. They die in the process."

"Father, I want a male child. Can we have sex without you impregnating me with a female seed?"

"Yes, that is not a problem," he responded.

"Then I would like that to happen. I will help my mother with her child, but I will not settle for anything but a son," she said, moving close to him.

"Come, I would like to show you everything," he said to her. If she really wanted a son by him, then he had to show her what she was up against.

He led her downstairs to Jane Wexler's quarters, showing her all the markers along the way. When they entered the room with the single chair, she didn't appear to be surprised.

"This is where you release yourself, isn't it?" she said, running her fingers over the chair.

"Jane, please come and meet my daughter," he called out to the android.

Jane appeared from behind the wall but didn't move forward.

"Wow, she is gorgeous. She isn't human, is she?" Jenny laughed softly.

"How can you tell?" he asked.

"No woman in the world could be that perfect," Jenny responded. She was obviously envious of the android's beauty.

"I made her many, many years ago. I use her to do research for me and as a receptacle for my sperm, my male sperm," he said matter-of-factly.

"Interesting—what does she do with it?"

"She is trying to get it to survive for more than twenty-four hours. Her goal is to get it to survive for thirty hours, giving her time to insert the sperm inside of a woman," he said.

"What is she made of?" Jenny asked.

"A special alloy from a meteor that hit the Earth a long time ago," he said.

"Can you make a body suit out of the alloy?"

"Yes, but that would only protect you from the outside—the heat on the inside would still burn you up," he said.

"Can I work with Jane?"

"Certainly," he told her.

"I like this chair. Can we try it?" Jenny eased into the chair.

Asmodais gave her hand a gentle squeeze. "Honey, I don't want to hurt you."

"Then don't hurt me. Just give me a sample so I know what I am getting myself in for," she said, beginning to undress. "Jane, would you please put these behind the wall?"

Jane took the clothes and moved behind the wall.

"Now, don't tell me you don't want a little piece of me," she said, giving him a tantalizing smile as she stretched out in the chair.

The room went dark, and he mounted her. He knew he couldn't go far, but he could at least give her a taste. He left the heat rise as he began to glow. She began to glow too.

"Is that too much?" he asked after a few seconds.

"No, a little more," she begged softly.

He went another ten seconds then shut the process down.

"How did I do?" she asked, with a twinkle n her eyes.

"You did well," he said, smiling at her as Jane brought back her clothes.

"But not even close, right?" She almost pouted at that idea.

"No, I was barely warm. I must be hotter than the sun when I erupt," he explained.

Jenny began putting on clothes. "Don't worry, Jane and I will figure a way to make it happen. Do you want to go back upstairs and do it the old-fashioned way?"

"I think that would be a good idea," he agreed.

The two of them returned to the main area and went to the master bedroom. They enjoyed conventional sex.

Samantha and Deacon Marsala Visit Winterhaven

The dinner Samantha Lee prepared for Deacon Marsala was outstanding. She was a better cook than he had thought she would be. After dinner, he decanted the bottle of wine from his car, and they drank it. It was a bottle of wine that he had brought over from Rome. She thought it was the best wine she had ever had. He thought it was a good red wine but not the best, a thought he didn't share with her.

When he suggested it was getting late and that he should be returning to the rectory, her smile told him that he wasn't leaving her apartment that night.

"You did say that you weren't practicing celibacy, right?" she asked.

"Yes, and I also stated that in the past I have enjoyed the pleasures of many women," he responded sipping more of his wine.

"Do you find me attractive?" she asked.

"Yes, I find you very attractive. I also find you a little scatterbrained." He laughed.

"Wait until you really get to know me. I am sure you will find me even more unconventional than most women. I normally wait until the second or third date before I allow a man to touch me, but I actually consider this our third date," she said.

"How do you figure that?" he asked.

"Well, the library was our first date, and dinner was our second date. So sitting out on the deck enjoying wine would be our third date by my definition. So sex is really not out of question for us. Of course, if you really want to go back to the rectory and miss having a good time tonight, then do as you wish." Samantha rose from the chair.

He followed her to the bedroom. The sex was better than the wine, much better. She was very active in the bed. She was not content to simply lay back and be the receiver of sex. Twice they reversed positions with her on the top sporadically. Later she had no problem allowing him to explore other parts of her body. It had been almost forever since he had enjoyed a woman so much.

The following morning, after she prepared him a good breakfast, she left for her office, and he drove directly to the Lynn estate. At the gate he told their security man that he was Deacon Marsala from the Hartford diocese, looking for a gift to help the needy. They allowed him to enter. Once he reached the house, Jerry and Michele Lynn were waiting for him on the porch.

"Deacon Marsala, it is good of you to come by. We did not meet at Mass on Sunday, but I recognize you from the introduction by the bishop," Jerry Lynn said to him.

The three of them went inside, and they ended up in the drawing room. One look at the woman, and he could see that glow about her.

He wanted to be polite and not spook her if she didn't know she was pregnant. "You have a certain glow about you. Is there congratulations in order?" he asked.

"Yes, but barely. How could you tell? I only found out yesterday," she asked, confused.

"As I said you have a glow that becomes you. Where is your daughter?" he asked.

"Jenny is away visiting friends," Jerry Lynn said, staring coldly at the man.

"Mrs. Lynn, since I know for a fact that the only man who has been in this house these last few days, other than your husband, is Asmodais Winters, I can only assume that the child implanted inside you is his. I cannot allow that seed to germinate and reach maturity. So you leave me no choice as to my next step," he said, as he pulled out his German Luger.

"Fuck you, Deacon," Jerry said and dove at Marsala. The man took the first bullet and fell to the floor immediately. The woman knelt beside her dead husband and stared up at him.

"You bastard, the Master will destroy you for this!" she yelled at him.

Before she could say more, he placed a new hole in her head one inch above the spot between her eyebrows. She fell onto her husband's body. Marsala had not wanted to kill the man; he had no choice about the woman. The VEF Command was explicit in dealing with women who had been impregnated by demons. They must not be allowed to gestate and introduce more demons into the world. She was carrying Asmodais's offspring. It was far too late to save her.

He contacted the VEF and told them what he had done. He explained the details to them the best that he could. They told him to get out of there, and they would deal with the locals through Interpol.

He quickly left the farm and drove back to town. He was back at the rectory when Samantha Lee called him an hour later.

"Did you have to kill both of them?" She sounded angry.

"They gave me no choice!"

"I will be by to pick you up in five minutes." It was an order, not a request.

"Are you arresting me?"

"Not yet. I have two visitors' passes to Winterhaven Security," she said and hung up.

Four minutes later she picked him up. She must have called him from her cell phone. They did not discuss the Lynn deaths. He was glad they didn't.

She showed their passes at the gate. Then an employee led them into the underground parking garage. Once there, two huge men guided them to the first floor, where Angela Blanco awaited them. She took them to a large, spacious office on the top floor. Marsala recognized her immediately as the woman he'd seen at the diner the day before. Fortunately she did not recognize him.

The office held a large desk next to a plate glass window overlooking the grounds. He noticed the heliport, but the space was empty at the time. He wondered if Asmodais had flown away. The room was surrounded on three sides with bookshelves filled with books and several doors that led to other adjacent rooms. There was a small desk in the far right corner of the room. They were seated before this desk.

He let Samantha do all the talking. She was the better communicator. Angela Blanco was all business as she explained some of the security measures in which the company was investing tons of research money at the time. Samantha asked if she could see the research lab, but Angela Blanco declined—a forty-eight-hour experiment was being performed. Perhaps at another time, with a little more notice, they might be able to tour the research facilities. Samantha said she would schedule a follow-up meeting with her.

Suddenly Marsala noticed confusion on the face of Angela Blanco. It was as if she recognized who he was. She worked for Asmodais. He would have warned her about him. She had been sent to get rid of him. Now she realized for the first time that she had failed in that mission.

"Time to go." Marsala gripped Samantha by the arm.

Samantha did not question his motive. She told Angela that she had another meeting to attend, and together the two of them made a hasty retreat from the compound.

Once they were off the premises, Marsala told her to make a sharp right, then another right, and park the car. She followed his directions and parked quickly. They both watched as a security vehicle from Winterhaven went by them.

"What was that all about?" She gave him a questioning glare.

"I was recognized. I saw the Blanco woman when my car was blown up yesterday. She had been sent to assassinate me. She didn't recognize me at first, but she did toward the end of the conversation. We got out of there in the nick of time. Five minutes later, we'd have never have made it out at all. Those clones shoot first and never ask questions," he said.

"What clones?" she asked.

"When we were heading up to the first floor, I saw two other men who looked exactly like those two who escorted us in. My bet is that they come in pairs."

"What did you think of Angela Blanco? Is she a clone?" Samantha asked.

"No, I don't think so," he said, staring out the front window.

"Do we need to get back in there?" she asked.

"Yes, but currently I don't see how that is possible. We are definitely not going to break into the place. I saw far too many monitors spread everywhere. Even if we netted the place, my bet is that they have backup systems even the FBI can only dream about," he said.

"Do you have a plan?" she asked.

"I am working on it," he said. "We have to stake out the place. My belief is that Angela and her husband are the only two people who have the run of the place and can come and go as they please. I am hoping that he is not as tough as she is. That kind of woman enjoys wearing the pants in the family."

Samantha laughed at that. "My ex-boyfriend said the same thing about me before I kicked his ass out of my apartment."

"I can imagine that was a great scene!" Marsala laughed too.

"Hey, there is Manny's Bar. I wonder if Blanco goes there." Samantha pointed to a bar across the street from where they were parked.

"It is possible. The bar is close to Winterhaven."

"Let's go visit Manny. I know him very well," she said and quickly jumped out of the car.

Marsala followed Samantha to the back of the unopened bar. She rapped three times on the door.

"We're not open! Come back in an hour," a male voice called from an intercom attached to the metal door.

"Manny, open up! I don't want to ask again or I'll take my ass elsewhere!" Samantha remonstrated.

A grinning Mexican-looking man opened the door. He looked to be in his late thirties. He was wearing a kitchen apron but no chef's hat. He was plump, but one could sense that all that weight was not mere fat.

Over the course of the next ten minutes, Marsala learned that Samantha and Manny had a fairly good working relationship, a lot of it based on her supplying him sex. Marsala didn't believe the FBI would allow her to compromise herself professionally and break contractual agreements and ethical codes. Sex is a card played in weakness; in most transactions, an FBI agent is acting from a position of strength. She would be able to claim favors from Manny just by letting his clientele know that she's with the FBI and hanging around. His town criminal element would not trouble him, and he could probably use the acquaintance to cut through any technicalities about liquor license or victualer's licenses. It would be fine if she was having sex with him because she likes him, likes sex, likes working-class guys, or anything of that kind. But she shouldn't be bribing him as a bartender with sex for information. If she needed street-level information, she should probably follow the time-honored and cost-effective method of paying a snitch. He would have to look into this activity more carefully. But he also learned that Blanco did visit the bar two or three times a week and often picked up women of the night for a few hours of relaxation. Blanco, if he maintained his schedule of visits to the bar, should return that night. Manny wanted Samantha to come alone, but she convinced him that Deacon Marsala was going to be joining her.

"Nice friend you have there," Marsala said as they got back into the car.

"An FBI agent is taught to use the locals as much as possible. Manny is a very good source of information. He has helped me with nine cases in the recent past. Of course, sometimes I stroke him but never in the line of duty or for specific information. We just are very good friends. I have lots of male friends that are not part of my FBI duty. You aren't a jealous priest, are you?" She hated having to explain herself to anyone. It was results that counted.

"I am not a priest," he laughed as they sped away.

"Let's keep that our own little secret for the time being. Now tell me why you killed the Lynn family."

"I had no choice. Asmodais Winters had corrupted the woman. He had sex with her and planted an evil seed inside her. The Vatican Elite Force Command is very strict about the steps to follow in cases like hers. I had not intended to kill the husband, but he jumped at me and I had no choice about shooting him. Killing her was my only mission once I knew that Asmodais had impregnated her," he said.

"What makes you think she didn't have sex with Asmodais before today? Maybe she's been spreading his contagion for all these years."

"No, he needed her to raise his daughter as her own. He could not have taken the chance on making her pregnant and having Jenny be treated as a second fiddle to his own child. It is possible they had sex, but not that she conceived."

"Okay, that makes sense. Is he that prolific?"

"I think he can control himself, but he has trouble doing it. Have your people identified that nun who died in the fire at the nunnery?"

She reported that dental work had proven the woman in the fire was not Sister Mary Alice. He told her that he surmised that Sister Alice was no longer a nun and was probably with Asmodais.

They returned to her apartment. They got very little rest that afternoon.

Marsala Exposed

Asmodais slapped Angela Blanco twice then yelled, "Your fucking security sucks!"

"Sir, we were able to confirm the woman was from the FBI. She had called in for an appointment. I had no reason to believe she would be working with Deacon Marsala. I thought he had been killed in the explosion. As soon as I recognized him, I alerted the staff to follow them when they left," she said humbly.

"And they fucking lost them! How the fuck could that happen?"

"I am looking into the programming," she tried to explain.

He stomped to his desk and stared at the computer for almost five minutes. When he turned to her and asked her how the cloning was progressing, he appeared to be calmer.

"My clone is currently functional, and we are working on a clone for Marvin. Both models should be available within two days," she responded.

"Well, that is something. At least you are making progress there. This thing with Marsala makes me annoyed, but not nervous yet. He is the best of the Vatican Elite Force. He is much better than anything they have thrown at me before. He killed the Lynn family with no compunction. He killed the altar boy with no compunction. He killed the stewardess without thinking. I am fortunate he didn't kill the woman and man in apartment

301. He is a killing machine. Fortunately he doesn't know about the other women. No doubt he would have done the same thing to my daughter and Alice if I had not gotten to them first. You are very fortunate to be alive yourself. Had he been with you alone in the conference room, we would not be talking right now," he said.

"We checked them both for weapons before they entered the building," she said softly.

That statement seemed to get Asmodais riled all over. "Marsala doesn't need a weapon to kill you. He *is* a weapon!"

"Yes, sir," she cowered.

"He has been here now. He has seen our security. No doubt he is making a plan of attack as we speak. He will discover a very devious plan, no doubt. We have to outthink him. Put that computer of yours to work downstairs. I need every possible way that he can get to us, and I mean *every* way, no matter how remote the possibility," he ordered.

"Yes, sir," she said but did not move away.

"Then why are you still here? Get your ass to the computer room and make it happen," he ordered.

"Yes, sir," she said and began to move toward the elevator leading from his office to the computer room.

"Send me one of your clones. I want to test it out personally," he called to her as she stepped into the elevator.

The elevator closed.

"What are you up to, Marsala? I know you have something up your sleeve. So now you have an ally in the FBI woman. That may be a fatal mistake," Asmodais said to himself.

The elevator opened, and out stepped a woman who appeared for all purposes to be Angela Blanco. Same proportions, same smile. No, the clone had a better body. He wondered if her husband was the one responsible for the modification. Probably so, Angela thought she was perfect already.

"What is your name, beautiful?" he asked, motioning for her to come to him.

"My name is A1. I am the first of ten models," the clone woman said, smiling as she approached. She explained her functions to him; they had been created primarily to serve his every need.

He asked her how she differed from the original, and she explained that she had been programmed with her human original's memories. However, her Positronic brain allowed her to make decisions much faster than her human counterpart could. Reaction times for A1, she told him, have been increased a hundredfold. She could perform any function of her human counterpart except procreation. When he asked if she could kill him, she responded that it was impossible to kill the master. However, she could kill anyone *for* the master, including her human original. When he asked her if she could fool Angela's husband, she said that she had already passed that test successfully. He ordered her to undress, and she obeyed without question. Had she been created with the special alloy? Yes, she said, she had.

When he ordered her to follow him into his bedroom, she picked up her clothes and obeyed him.

Marvin Blanco

Marsala and Samantha Lee arrived at Manny's restaurant bar shortly after seven and were escorted into Manny's office. They could see the bar from a one-way surveillance mirror. Blanco was in the bar talking to a customer.

Samantha was wearing a very short skirt and a tight blouse that Marsala thought a little too revealing, but she had insisted on wearing the outfit just in case she had to go into action. He could not figure what kind of action she would be looking for on a stakeout, but he relented after he saw her in the outfit. He wore his normal dark suit.

He watched the people in the bar through the mirror. She sat beside him for a few minutes then stood up when Manny joined them.

The bar seemed to cater to the locals. It wasn't a large place. There was a long serving counter with seven stools along the customer side. Behind the counter were two spigots for draft beer and three large glass-fronted refrigerators for cold drinks. A wine rack containing a variety of red and white wines was on a wall rack behind the bar. Along the side of the rear counter was an assortment of liquors and spirits. A sink was filled with ice to serve those people who wanted their drinks on the rocks.

A tall woman was behind the bar. She was not Mexican, like he would have expected from a Mexican bar, but she appeared to know her way around the bar and know the few customers who were seated on the stools. There were seven tables, all seating four comfortably.

Marsala didn't see a separate waitress for the tables, so either the woman behind the bar would visit the tables or the customers would be required to come to the counter to order drinks.

When they entered the office, Marsala had counted only five customers, two were at the bar and three at one of the tables. The only woman in the bar was the bartender.

Manny joined them in the office a few minutes after eight, leaving the woman to tend to the few customers in the bar area. Manny spoke to Samantha and probably kissed her behind Marsala's back.

Marsala continued to face forward. Something told him that Samantha had plans of her own, and that at this point in time, they didn't include him. He heard her make a small, contented sound from behind him. He dared not look.

Meanwhile, Samantha Lee forced herself not to have sex with Manny. It was a difficult decision, but one she thought appropriate at this period of time. How many times had the two of them had sex? She recalled at least eight times. Manny was strictly an ass man. Sure, he had fucked her normally a couple of times, but he much preferred the domineering role from behind. She didn't mind. She was on assignment, and Manny had provided the coverage for them. Manny deserved more than merely a thank-you. But it was not to be. Tomorrow she might stop by early in the morning and give him a royal thank-you but not tonight.

Would Marsala be jealous if she gave Manny a piece of ass? He shouldn't be. She was taking care of him at the apartment. In any case, in a few days, Marsala would be gone; she would still be here. She needed to maintain her friends. If letting Manny fuck her in the ass maintained the friendship, then so be it.

The three of them made small talk while they waited for Blanco to appear at the bar.

It was around nine when Marvin Blanco arrived at the bar. He smiled and waved to all the locals then sat at the end of the bar. He appeared to be waiting for someone.

"He's waiting for the women to appear. They should start coming in shortly," Manny said, pointing the man out to Marsala.

Samantha handed Marsala an earpiece. "Plug this in and listen." He plugged in the earpiece. Then she turned back to Manny.

"Come on, Manny, you are going to introduce me to Blanco."

Before Marsala could object, the couple left the room. A few seconds later, Samantha and Manny appeared on the other side of the mirror. She took the empty barstool next to Blanco. Marsala didn't like that, but he could no more control her than he could control Asmodais.

He overheard the introductory conversation between Samantha and Blanco. She was doing her best to become Blanco's friend for the evening. Blanco was an MIT graduate and proud of the work he was doing for Winterhaven, which mainly consisted of making clones or androids for security purposes.

Samantha admitted to Blanco that she was an FBI agent but said that she was not at the bar on FBI work, but to enjoy the evening. Blanco appeared to buy her spiel; he seemed to become more relaxed.

When she asked Blanco if he could make a clone of her, Blanco told her he could do it with no problem at all. However, she would have to go to the Winterhaven facility and pose for him. He couldn't make a model out of thin air. She explained that the woman she met earlier that day would not allow her to be alone with him in the facility. Blanco had laughed and told her that the woman was his wife but he could get her into his lab without his wife knowing about it.

Blanco's pager went off. "Shit!" he whispered. The world changed right before Marsala's eyes.

"What's wrong?" she asked when he shut off his pager.

"I have to leave. My latest experiment has a problem that requires my attention," Blanco said, obviously upset by the page.

Samantha thought quickly. This could be the best chance she had to get to the compound. Marsala would have to adjust from behind the mirror. "Do you want me to go with you?" she asked.

He stared at her for a few seconds. He obviously wanted her, and she probably might not be there when he returned. In fact, he might never see her again. "She is not there. We could start the clone process tonight."

"Can you get me inside? You do have a lot of security systems in place, you know."

"No problem. I can override the system. I can get you in and out in thirty minutes," he said.

"Will I have my clone when I leave?" she asked, hoping the answer was positive so she wouldn't have to see him again.

"No, it takes roughly twenty-two hours to complete the cloning process."

Samantha squeezed his leg. "So if I go with you now, then you can start the cloning process, and this time tomorrow night, we can be enjoying ourselves *and* the clones?"

"All right, but we have to go right now," he said, rising and tossing a fifty on the bar.

Marsala had already started moving. He didn't like how this was going down, but there was little he could do to change anything—or was there? He almost ran downstairs and out the back door. He had barely closed the trunk of Blanco's car when he heard the two of them get into the car. He was committed now. If the security guards caught him, his ass was dead, but he couldn't let Samantha Lee do this trip alone.

Asmodais Seeks Help

Asmodais had trusted Angela to take care of Marsala, and that had obviously not worked. He needed a new set of eyes on the problem. Marsala had taken refuge in the rectory, so why not attack him from within? He left the compound in his secure limo and headed to the rectory. On the way he called Bishop Davies, who was still in the Stamford area, and told him to be at the rectory and supply him with an audience.

Upon his arrival he noticed the bishop's limo parked in the designated car space. Good, the bishop was ready to receive his new orders from him.

As he exited the limo, a young priest was there to open the door and usher him inside the main office building. At the threshold, the young man bowed his head and announced that Asmodais Winters was there. Asmodais did not bow to the bishop. He had never bowed to humans and wasn't about to start.

Off duty, the bishop wore a dark suit and clerical collar rather than his cassock. He was, however, sitting in a very large, expensive chair befitting his title.

Marsala waited until the bishop waved all the others out of the room. He approached the bishop when they were alone.

"How can I assist you?" Davies asked.

"This Deacon Marsala has become a thorn in my side. I wish him to be eliminated immediately," Asmodais ordered.

"Sir, not even a bishop has authority over the Vatican Elite Force agents. They are part of Interpol. We can only support their efforts, and in no way can we delay or deter them from their assignments," Davies said calmly.

"This church and these grounds all belong to me. I supplied them to the Church over fifty years ago at no cost. I pay the taxes, and I pay the maintenance. I also have the lien on your property in Hartford. Now, according to our agreement, I can retake this land and everything on it at any time I so desire. If I do not see Marsala eliminated within twenty-four hours, then I will recall everything. Do I make myself perfectly clear?" Asmodais said without hesitation.

"The Vatican will reimburse you for the land," Davies said nervously.

"By the time the Vatican gets involved, this area will be sold to make hotels and brothels for my people. I will take your altar boys and your nuns and put them to work as whores and prostitutes. And you know I can do it too, especially with your nuns." Asmodais laughed.

"What must I do?" Davies asked in a defeated tone.

"Eliminate and kill Marsala. It is as simple as that. You do that one assignment for me, and you may continue to survive in this remote corner of the world. Fail me, and your little world falls apart in an instant," Asmodais said in an angry tone.

"If I do this, my support from Rome will be severely limited," the bishop said.

"I don't give a shit about your problems with Rome or the Vatican. Are you going to do this or not?" Asmodais almost screamed at the weak man.

"Yes, but it will take a few days to have the forces together," Davies responded softly.

"You don't have a few days. You have twenty-four hours."

"I will need the full twenty-four hours," the bishop said.

"Twenty-four hours it is, and not a second longer. If it is not completed by then, you can kiss this place good-bye, and your staff too," Asmodais said calmly.

"It will be done," Davies muttered.

"Good," Asmodais said and was smiling for the first time. "I'm a little short on my quota of pregnant females. I could use a little of your support for getting back on track. You know how angry Iblis can get when I miss my quotas."

"How can I help you there?" Davies asked.

"I would like to spend the afternoon with a few of your nuns, especially the Mother Superior. Iblis gives me extra credit when I get nuns pregnant," Asmodais explained.

"I can't give you permission to have children with the nuns," Davies said.

"Either you give me your permission, or the twenty-four hours is reduced to six hours, after which I will have them anyway," Asmodais said.

"How many do you want?" Davies asked.

"I want five this afternoon and three in the morning. I want the Mother Superior first, and she will not be counted in the eight. She can be helpful with getting the consent of the others," Asmodais responded.

"Mother Superior will not consent," Davies said softly.

"Just put us together. She will consent to me. She is a woman, isn't she? I can control women with no problem. Why do you care about them anyway? It is not like I am taking another altar boy from you. By the way, the altar boy on Easter Sunday was delicious. It has been a long time since I found such an agreeable young boy. It is too bad that Marsala killed him. He would have made a great convert for Sitri." Asmodais grinned. Sitri was the demon of homosexuality.

The bishop pressed the intercom on his desk and requested that Mother Superior come to his chambers. He did not explain why he wanted her, and no one asked.

Asmodais told the bishop he had a lot of planning to do and only twenty-four hours to execute his plan. The bishop should leave and make arrangements. The bishop left just as Mother Superior entered.

She looked confused—she was in the bishop's quarters, and the bishop was leaving. He had never left her alone in the inner sanctuary in the past. She was pleased when she saw that only Asmodais was in the room.

Asmodais gave her an evil grin and motioned for her to come to him.

"It has been a while since I was with you last," he said, running his hands over her arms.

"Yes, it was almost twenty years ago when you came to me after being with Sister Alice. I have been watching over her for you. I was hoping that you would seek me out before you left again," Mother Superior said, smiling up at him.

"You have done an excellent job with her. I needed you to concentrate on her growth and not have a child of your own at that time. But now it is your time to fulfill your destiny," he said as he began to help her out of her habit.

She was not nearly as good as Alice had been, but then Alice had been much younger the first time they had been together. He found her as receptive as she had been many years ago.

"What happened to Sister Alice?" she asked as she arose from the carpeted floor without her clothes.

"Alice is no longer a nun. She resides with me and is having a second child," he responded.

"How else can I serve the Master this afternoon?"

"You can supply me with five more nuns this afternoon and three in the morning. Do you think you can do that?" he said to her. "They must be of childbearing age. I don't want to waste my sperm on old bitches."

"Then can I assume that I am with child?" She looked pleased at the prospect.

"If not now, you will be before tomorrow afternoon."

"Then I must find young nuns who are not committed to their religious vows and can be turned. I will supply the sisters that you request," she said calmly.

"And I want you to watch while I devour them."

"Yes, Master, I will go now and bring you in the first sister in a few minutes," she said and left.

Bishop Davies made two telephone calls. The first was to an ex-altar boy, John Ester, who was now a young man working for a construction firm. Davies knew the man was totally dedicated to him and had been since they met when the boy was ten, which had been more than ten years ago. He told the young man he had a personal job for him. The man said he would be at the rectory shortly.

The second call was to Father Bennet, his second-in-command in Hartford. He explained the situation to Bennet and requested his assistance in assassinating Marsala. Bennet said he would be in Stamford in a few hours and oversee the entire plan.

Bishop Davies presided over the six o'clock Mass and noted that all the nuns were present for the Mass. Mother Superior was there too, but they didn't speak. He hoped that she had allowed Asmodais to have his way with her. It had been a while since he had enjoyed her company in her cell at the rectory in Stamford. Once Asmodais had left, the bishop would visit her again. Perhaps he would even invite her up to Hartford for a few days.

Deacon Marsala was not at the Mass, but he knew Bennet had seen the man on Easter Sunday when he had been with him at Mass. Bennet would identify the man to John Ester, the ex-altar boy. Bennet and Ester disappeared after Mass. He could only pray for the sake of the Church and the nuns that the death of Marsala could be achieved swiftly. This had to be done within twenty-four hours.

Jenny Works with Jane

Jenny Lynn touched Jane's skin. It felt like real skin, but she knew it wasn't. If the skin was resistant to very high heat, then it could not be real skin. She asked Jane how the skin was made, and Jane told her it was from a special alloy that only the Master knew of. Jenny asked if a body suit could be made for her so she could watch when Jane and Asmodais had sex. The android explained that protection could be provided for the outside of her body but the internal parts would not be protected.

Jenny then wanted to know what happened to the sperm generated by Asmodais. Jane explained the process of collecting the sperm and placing it in specially treated dark glass vials so that the sperm would not lose the heat.

"The sperm lives twenty hours currently, five hours after delivery, it has cooled enough that it can be inserted into a woman's womb. My goal has been to maintain the sperm for thirty hours. Once I can reach thirty hours, then the sperm can be released after five hours and a full twenty four hours can be used to impregnate the female egg," the robot reported.

"What if, after five hours, a female egg was implanted inside you? Could you keep the fertilized egg alive long enough to re-implant the egg in me after twenty-four hours?" Jenny asked.

"I do not have the proper fluids inside of me to cause the eggs to become fertilized."

"When your body heats up to match his heat, does everything inside you reach the same temperature?" Jenny asked.

"My womb matches the heat."

"No, that is not my question," Jenny said, irritated. "Does your entire body reach that temperature? For example, do your kidneys reach the same temperature as the external parts of your body?"

"I have no kidneys. The answer is no. There are several internal spots inside my body that are protected from the heat and are not affected by the outside temperature. A coolant circulates to keep my inner parts from burning out."

"Could you keep my egg and my fluids protected for the full five hours inside your body?"

"Yes, that is possible," Jane said.

"Then, after the five hours, when the heat has been reduced, can you release my fluids, then when the time comes re-implant the egg inside of me?" Jenny asked.

"My internal clock would have to be readjusted," Jane said.

"Now tell me all the things that could go wrong with the plan," Jenny said.

"If the fluid is released too soon, the sperm will deteriorate too quickly and become useless. If the heat is too high when the sperm cells are introduced, then the egg will be destroyed. If my coolant ports are opened at the wrong time, then my body will be destroyed from the inside out," Jane explained.

"Those are extremely high risks, but they're manageable. Is there any way to protect my internal organs from the heat?" Jenny asked.

"The master attempted such a program many years ago, but the test failed. The body was able to withstand the heat, but the woman became a complete vegetable. The egg died because of improper attention by the woman. The experiment was never tried again."

"Why do you think she became a vegetable?" Jenny asked.

"The body can be shielded from almost anything but the brain is the most sensitive organ in the body. The heat made the brain react very negatively, and it was never the same again."

"You must have known this might happen. Why didn't you offer more protection for her brain?" Jenny asked.

"We had adequate protection for the physical brain. The female brain did not feel the heat directly. The problem was that the brain has a protection mechanism of its own that takes over in dire situations. It literally shuts down when it feels impending danger. We tried to fool the brain but were unsuccessful, and the master said the risk was too high. We have not tried again," Jane said.

"How long does it take to readjust the body with all the protection?" Jenny asked.

"It takes four sessions to adjust the body and add the protection. Each session can last up to four hours."

"Okay, here is what we are going to do. Plan A is to prepare you for my egg and fluids. Plan B, which we will do at the same time, is to prepare me for the master," Jenny said, smiling at the android.

Jane agreed to prepare herself for the assimilation of the female egg and the fluids. She would begin the preparation to prepare Jenny's body with the four sessions.

Jenny left Jane and went to the main living quarters. She found her father in the master bedroom shower. She slipped off her clothes and joined him.

"How are you doing with Jane?" he asked.

"Very well, but it is too early yet to tell you our plans," Jenny said.

"Good, I hoped I would find you both here," a female voice said.

They turned and smiled when Alice joined them in the shower.

"Family time," Alice said, smiling at them both.

Samantha Gets Cloned

"There, that should do it," Marvin Blanco said as he pushed a button on a small keypad when they approached the compound.

Samantha Lee cuddled next to him across the bench seat. She had not expected he would actually bring her to the compound that night. She thought she would have to work on him a few days before he broke down and invited her. She wondered what had happened to Marsala.

The underground garage opened, and the vehicle moved inside. There were no guards to greet them.

She asked about the guard, hoping that she was still in range of Marsala if he were following them. Blanco explained that the clones were in rest mode. He had turned them off for a while, but external security was still on.

The two of them left the car and went to an elevator.

Marsala crept out of the trunk and waited behind the car until they were in the elevator. He watched the numbers on the top of the elevator begin going down. He waited for the numbers to stop before he moved toward the doors. They had gone to the basement. He pressed the button for the elevator to return to the garage area. He hoped the guards were really in rest mode.

He eased into the elevator and pressed the basement button. The doors closed, and he began his descent toward the basement.

He listened through his earpiece as Samantha kept him informed as to what was going on with her and Blanco.

"Follow me closely and don't touch anything. These computers feed information to the clones inside the building. The computers are very sensitive to the touch," Blanco warned her.

Marsala noted the warning as he got off the elevator.

Samantha noticed that the elevator had moved back up to the garage level and was moving down again. Had Marsala been able to bypass all that security and get into the compound, or was someone else joining them? She dared not answer her own questions.

She followed Blanco into another room that looked like a large x-ray machine. "What is that?"

"That is the cloning room," he said, smiling to her as he moved to a large monitor.

She watched as he pressed a few buttons on a computer console.

"It was just a faulty address. My experiment is back on target. Now take off your clothes," He explained that she needed to be completely naked for the process to work.

It took her a few seconds to remove all her clothes. She left her transceiver pinned to her panties. It was so small that it was barely noticeable. She hoped the messages were getting through to Marsala.

"You are beautiful. I don't think I am going to have to make very many modifications to you at all," he said, letting his eyes roam over her naked body.

"Please feel free to make any modifications you like, but it still has to basically look like me. There are a lot of men I need to fool."

"Okay, step into the chamber and think wonderful thoughts. This should take no more than a few minutes to initiate. Once it has started, then it takes another ten minutes before the replication has completed," he ordered. "You only need to be still for a few seconds during the first scan. For everything to work perfectly, you should be perfectly relaxed. I promise it won't hurt a bit. I have tried it on myself. All the male clones were made from my body. Of course they were greatly enhanced physically to meet the requirements of security."

Marsala moved silently through the computers in the outer room. He could hear the voices of Samantha and Blanco in another room via the earpiece. He finally found the room and concealed himself behind one of the computers. He spotted the naked body of Samantha inside the chamber and saw the laser lights as they passed over her body.

"Perfect, honey, you are doing great," Blanco called to her. "Now open yourself up a little more, bend over, spread your cheeks, and open your mouth."

Marsala watched as Samantha did what the man ordered her to do. Her body was completely immersed in a bright blue light. At first Marsala thought she had completely disappeared and that Blanco had destroyed her body. Then, just as quickly, the light turned green, and he saw her again.

Samantha spotted Marsala hiding in the background. She gave him a quick wink then turned back to Blanco.

"It is done. You can come out now," Blanco called to her.

The green light went off, and Samantha stepped out of the small room. She reached for her clothes and began to slip them on. She was determined not to give Blanco anything until she had the clone.

"How long?"

"Ten minutes, then both of them will be ready to be manufactured. Then, tomorrow night, you will have your clone," he said to her.

"Both of them?"

"Yes, one for you and one for me." Blanco began pulling her close.

"Tomorrow night the original will be all yours." Samantha was going to do her best to lead him on. Tomorrow night would be soon enough without jeopardizing her reputation. Blanco just might stop the project as soon as he was back in the lab after having her. She had to hold herself in reserve to ensure he would follow through. He had seen her naked. She knew he wanted her.

He asked her why she had put her clothes back on, and she explained that time was limited and that he only got the one shot tonight. If the process didn't work, then she would return another time. He had laughed and told her the process would work. He wanted a sample of the original. She told him that as soon as she was assured the process had worked, she would gladly give him a sample.

There was silence for ten minutes. Blanco kept monitoring the computers and Samantha stood near his side. Marsala waited patiently behind the computers.

Ten minutes passed, and a bell sounded.

"The cooking starts now," Blanco said, leaving Samantha and turning to the monitor. He pressed several keys on the computer keyboard. "*Voila.*"

"Then I guess it is time for me to go. Will you take me back to the club?" she asked.

"As soon as I get my sample of the original."

"When you bring my clone tomorrow night, you will get a piece of the original. You have seen enough of me tonight." Samantha tried for a teasing smile.

"Okay, I will be happy to bring the clones to you tomorrow night, but I want a piece of the original on delivery."

While Samantha and Blanco haggled, Marsala headed quickly to the elevator and upstairs. He was inside Blanco's trunk when the two arrived. He slipped out of the car when it parked at Manny's while Samantha was taking care that Blanco did not see him. Blanco left almost immediately.

"That was scary, very scary," Marsala said when they were alone.

"What choice did I have? Come on, let's get out of here. I need to go back to my apartment and take a hot shower and get that slime off me." Samantha herded him into her car.

The Bishop's Attack

Marsala wanted to stop by the rectory and get another change of clothes before returning to spend the night with Samantha Lee. He had insisted on returning to the rectory alone, but she would have none of it. She followed him in her own car from a safe distance.

As he approached the rectory, he thought it was strange that most of the lights around the sleeping quarters were all out. In the two nights he had spent there since he came to America, the lights had not been out.

"Are you okay?" Samantha whispered into his earpiece, noting that he'd slowed almost to a stop.

He told her he didn't like the fact that the area surrounding the sleeping quarters was unlit. Perhaps this was a setup for another ambush? Samantha told him to give her at least two minutes before he drove inside the rectory parking lot. She had night goggles in her car and would check things out for him.

Samantha parked at the diner across the street from the rectory, then quickly crossed the street and moved silently through the manicured yard toward the dark sleeping quarters. She had followed Marsala to the area the day before when she left for work. Using her special glasses, she soon discovered the two men hiding near the entrance to Marsala's room.

"I have two suspects waiting for you. One has a rifle, and the other is carrying a very large knife," she reported to Marsala.

"When I drive in, can you take out the one with the rifle?" he asked.

She told him she could take out both of them if he wanted her to. He told her he needed to capture one of them, preferably the one with the knife. He explained that the one with the gun was probably a hired killer and had come prepared to kill him. The other one had come to the scene ill-prepared and was probably a novice. The second one would be more likely to talk than the first one. She had to agree with his logic. She would have to remember that logic the next time she was attacked by a man with a knife. She clicked on her silencer. The last thing they needed was for either assailant to hear the noise and flee the scene before he could be captured.

When Marsala pulled his car into the area, the men separated, not wanting to be detected in the lights of the car before they completed their mission.

As soon as the man with the gun was out of sight of his comrade, Samantha dropped him with a single shot. He fell silently to the ground. She then turned her attention toward Marsala and the other man. She watched as Marsala climbed out of the vehicle as if nothing was going on. The man crept closer on Marsala's blind side behind the car and on the passenger's side.

"He is coming up from behind you from behind the car. He is about to lunge at you," she called softly to Marsala.

She watched as Marsala moved more quickly than she had thought he could possibly move. With a quick turn, the situation was at his advantage. A right-cross from Marsala, and the man tumbled to the ground. The man had never seen the fist at all until it was too late. Samantha streaked across the grounds just as Marsala was hoisting the man to his shoulder. She followed the two inside Marsala's designated quarters. She handcuffed the man and sat him in a chair in the room.

"Now let's see how talkative he is," Marsala said as he threw a picture of water into the young man's face.

The young man awoke instantly and stared up at Marsala and Samantha Lee.

"Why were you trying to kill me?" Marsala asked calmly.

The young man looked toward the door.

"I took care of your friend with the gun. He won't be coming to your rescue," Samantha said.

"He is not my friend. He is a priest and a friend of the bishop," the young man said softly.

"Why does the bishop want to kill me?" Marsala asked, taking a seat and sitting directly in front of the man in handcuffs.

"I don't know. The other one said it had to do with something about you wanting to destroy the Church and the bishop. The bishop asked me to help the man. I had no choice. The bishop ordered me to assist the man," the beaten young man said.

"What were you supposed to do when the job was completed?" Marsala asked.

"I have a number I was to call and leave a message that the job was done. The number is in my shirt pocket," the potential assassin whispered.

Samantha retrieved the paper and glanced at it. "This has the Hartford area code and city code."

Marsala retrieved the cell phone from the young man. "You will leave a message that the job is done and that the other man is getting rid of the body," Marsala ordered as he dialed the number and placed the phone next to the young man's ear. He held the cell phone so that all three of them could hear what was being said.

"Bishop Davies speaking," the person answered on the other end of the line.

The young man repeated what Marsala had ordered him to say.

"Very good, John. You can come in for confession tomorrow, and I will absolve you personally. Go home now, and I will see you tomorrow," Bishop Davies said and hung up.

Marsala closed the cell phone then ripped out the battery. "Can you take him into custody without fanfare?" he asked Samantha.

"Yes, but what are you going to do?" she asked.

"I must make myself scarce for at least a few hours. I should go see the bishop tomorrow. Can I stay at your place tonight?" Marsala said.

"You know you can stay with me. There is a key to my apartment pinned to the birdfeeder in the backyard. Sorry, I had to move it there to hide it from my last lover."

They separated, and she took the young man to FBI headquarters. She told the man on duty that she wanted him locked up for a full twenty-four hours without anyone knowing it. The FBI agent on duty followed her orders.

She then returned to her apartment and found Marsala waiting for her.

"What is Asmodais going to do next to get rid of me? He tried his goons, and now he had tried the Church. We have to get him before he is successful. Twice he has made a mistake. I don't think he will be making a third mistake," he said.

"Come on, let's go to bed. This has been an eventful day. We need some rest," she said as she took his hand and led him to the bedroom.

"You know I would have been dead had you not been with me tonight," he said, pulling her into his arms.

"Yes, you do seem to make a lot of enemies."

"I only have one enemy who's trying to kill me. As soon as we eliminate him, then we can go on living," he said.

"Well, no one is going to kill you again tonight. Let's go to bed." Samantha began to undress.

The next morning Marsala left for Hartford, and Samantha Lee went to take care of the prisoner in FBI headquarters. They agreed to meet at Manny's that night to see if Blanco had been able to produce the clone for her.

Marsala entered the Hartford Rectory around noon and slipped by the guards easily. He entered the confessional and notified the priest on duty that his name was John and that the bishop had promised to hear his confession personally. The priest was gone a few minutes, then someone replaced him in the confessional booth.

"Thank you for coming, John. I have prayed for your soul all night. God has heard my pleas for forgiveness and has told me to relay to you that all is forgiven," the bishop said softly.

"Thank you, Bishop, for your forgiveness, but now my question is who will forgive you," Marsala said then moved quickly from his side to the back side of the bishop's entry to the confessional booth. He opened the curtain and stared down at the man. He was holding a very large butterfly knife that had been assigned to him during his VEF training days.

"You! But you are supposed to be dead! You being alive will spoil everything!" the bishop said, staring up at him.

"Sorry, Bishop, but I don't take death so lightly. You have two minutes to tell me what is going on, or I will kill you where you sit," Marsala said firmly but softly.

"Asmodais Winters owns all the land of the Church in this area. He had threatened to pull back all his holdings and make whores and prostitutes of the nuns if you are still alive by three o'clock this afternoon," Bishop Davies explained.

"You idiot, Asmodais can do no such thing. The Vatican bought this land from the State ten years ago. He has no lien on the property. What else have you done for him?" Marsala asked.

"He wanted eight nuns plus Mother Superior. I thought he had control over everything. I couldn't allow him to take over the church. I gave him what he asked for," the bishop said.

"You are not worthy to be a bishop," Marsala mumbled then rammed the blade of the knife deep into the bishop's chest. The bishop never made a sound. He left the bishop in the confessional booth and drove aware from the rectory. He was disappointed in the development of things. He called the Vatican Elite Force Command and told them what he had done. It was up to them to clean up this mess. He still had to deal with Asmodais Winters.

On his way back to Stamford, he called Samantha Lee. She was in a tizzy. Someone had broken into her apartment and ransacked it. The person had also marked up her walls and stolen her clothes. He told her to meet him in Bridgeport at the first service area across the bridge from Milford. She was there when he arrived. They filled up the tank then parked to make plans for the night.

The Clones Arrive

Marvin Blanco smiled as the two clones walked out of the incubation chamber. Damn, he had to admit to himself that he did great work. They looked outstanding. They had all the modifications he had plugged into the formula early that morning. He just had to sample the models just like he had sampled all the other female clones before turning one over to Angela.

He grabbed one of them by the arm and took her to his sleeping quarters. Thankfully Angela was not there and had not been in the lab all day. He guessed that was one of the benefits of the big boss being in town; Angela spent a lot of time with him, so he could get a lot more work done in the lab. Twenty minutes later he decided the clone really was better than the original. There was no way a human could move the way the clone moved. Sure, he would still give her the other clone, but he didn't need the original tonight. Perhaps he would never need her again unless he wore the clone out. He had used the special alloy when building the clones, though, so he doubted the model would ever wear out.

He switched the security clones into rest mode and left the complex in a rush. He wanted to get back to his garage and continuing playing with his model of the FBI agent.

Around nine o'clock, Samantha and Marsala were waiting in Manny's parking lot for Blanco to arrive. Marsala was hidden, but she was waiting in open view for the man. He was right on schedule, and in the backseat were two females that looked exactly like Samantha. She was more than amazed at the clones.

"God, I thought you were really not going to be able to clone me. Damn, they look just like me," Samantha said as one of the clones got out of the car.

"Am I a good chef or what?" Blanco said as he motioned for the other clone to come up to the front seat of his car.

"You are a great chef. This one is for me?" she asked.

"Yes," he said.

"Will she take orders from me?" Samantha asked.

"Absolutely," Blanco told her.

"Can you make more of me?" she asked.

"Not without you being present," he said. "The model must be present each time. We can't make a clone of a clone yet."

The clone of Samantha Lee stood next to her silently.

"I have to leave. My wife will be home shortly, and I need my clone of you in the garage lab before she gets home," Blanco said. He was lying. The truth was that he had sampled his clone and found her much delectable than the original could ever be. He wanted to get home and enjoy her before Angela got home.

"Yes, you should go, but before you leave, I do owe you something, I believe," Samantha said.

He glanced at his watch. "Sorry I don't have time, catch you later." He sped away.

Marsala joined Samantha and the female clone. "How do I know which one is which?"

"I am sure we will work all that out." Samantha took the hand of the clone. "Let's get out of here."

"My thoughts exactly."

The clone sat in the back of the car while they sped down the highway toward Samantha's apartment. Marsala wondered about something.

"Who is Asmodais Winters?" he asked the clone.

"Asmodais Winters is the father of us all," the clone responded softly.

Samantha Lee turned toward him with a confused look.

"I thought this might be the case. Blanco could only code what was given to him to code. Asmodais is the real maker of the cloning process. We have to be very careful with her," he said to Samantha. "Can you turn her off?"

She reached into her skirt pocket and pressed a button on a small device. "Blanco gave me this last night after you left. It controls her. This will also turn off all the other ones when I come to see him again," she said.

"You are never going back into that place alone again," he said sternly.

"I know. I was really glad to see you there."

"I'm surprised you didn't haul his ass out of the car and have sex with him tonight anyway, or did Miss Clone wear him out before he got here?"

"You do really have a problem! I do whatever it takes to get results. Sometimes the only thing I have working for me is my body, and when that's the case, I use it. You have to get over this jealous streak of yours. I have been very nice to you and given more of myself to you than I have most men. But I have a job to do around here. Soon your job will be completed or you will be dead, and either way I will still be here alone. I have to think of my future too," she said raising her voice as she turned into the apartment complex. She had forgotten that her apartment had been all but destroyed.

"I don't think this is a good place to spend the night. Do you have another place that we could go?" he asked.

"I have a friend in Greenwich that I haven't seen for a long time, but I don't think you want to go there. My friend enjoys sex with me a little too much," she said sarcastically.

"Perhaps we could drop the clone off there," he retorted.

"I wouldn't want her broken the first night."

"Let's go to the nunnery, then. I can slip her into my quarters without anyone knowing she is there. If someone does find her, she can tell them she is a visiting nun," he suggested. "Turn her back on for a second."

She flipped the ON switch.

"Can you pretend to be a nun for a few days?" he asked the clone.

"Yes," the clone responded.

"You will be a nun in all respects for the next few days. You will be under a vow of silence and remain in your quarters until we return for you. Once inside your quarters, you will go into REST mode and remain that way until we return. Do you understand?" he said calmly.

"Yes," the clone responded.

"Turn her off," he said.

Samantha followed his direction.

They drove silently to the nunnery, where he stashed the clone in the room. He told her that if anyone came by, she was to write a message that she was doing penance. If a nun came by, she was to request clothes via a written message. He considered taking her with him and stashing her in a closet and turning her off. But this appeared to be a better plan, at least for the moment—visitors rooms were rarely checked.

He and Samantha found a motel in Ridgefield, Connecticut, and after a shower they went to bed.

Marvin Blanco Erased

Angela Blanco was already at home when her husband came into the driveway. She watched as he went to his garage workshop before coming inside. When deep into a project, he would often spend the night in the garage. However, now she would have sworn that she saw someone enter the garage with him, a female-shaped someone.

She knew her husband enjoyed women and often slept with them after a long day at the office, but he never brought them home. He would normally stop by a local motel to take care of that kind of business then come home alone. To her knowledge, he had never brought a woman home with him.

She waited a few minutes, then her curiosity got the better of her. She walked silently to the garage and slipped in, unheard. She heard the sounds of sex in progress. She took her time and eased around the room. Then she saw the woman.

She stared in disbelief. It was the FBI agent, Samantha Lee, the very same woman who had been to Winterhaven with Deacon Marsala yesterday. The woman was completely naked and allowing her husband to plunder her.

"Yes, baby, that is exactly what I like," the FBI agent was moaning.

"Is that deep enough?" Blanco asked.

"Any deeper, baby, and it would come out the other end," the woman flattered him and was urging him on.

Angela stared. This couldn't be happening. There was no way the FBI agent would be so agreeable with her husband, and she doubted the woman would ever call him *baby*. No, there was definitely something wrong with this scene.

"Marvin, what the fuck are you doing?" Angela said as she came out from her hiding place.

"Enjoying a nice piece of FBI ass," Blanco laughed. "Honey, this is my wife," he said to the woman beneath him.

The woman smiled up at her. "It is good to meet you, ma'am. Your husband is a fabulous fuck."

"You cloned that FBI woman, didn't you?" Angela said, having realized that this creature could not be the FBI agent.

"Hey, it was her idea," Blanco laughed as he withdrew from the clone.

"Asmodais is going to be totally pissed. He will kill us both," Angela said nervously.

"Then don't tell him. I'll keep her locked up in my garage," Marvin said. He seemed to think this simple tactic would solve all their problems.

She was livid. She knew Asmodais would review all the security tapes. She felt a little better when Marvin convinced her that he had taken precautions with all the security. She was nervous about A1 detecting the security defects. However, Asmodais hadn't paged her. Maybe he didn't know anything.

She stared at the clone. It was one of Blanco's best works. She wondered how close to original it really was. She asked about the clone of him, and he told her that there had been a glitch earlier that evening, but he had fixed it. His clone should be ready by the time they got to work the next morning.

"Did you at least fuck the FBI agent?" she asked.

"No, but she can't be nearly as good as the clone. I made her supersensitive in all the right areas. You should try her, honey, I think you will enjoy her," he said.

"I'm not a dyke!" Angela laughed, but her eyes were still glued to the female body.

"You don't have to be a dyke. She can be the dyke. She can be anything you want her to be. You give her a command, and she'll follow it to the letter with no questions asked. She can do it all."

"She does look beautiful," Angela said as she neared the clone.

"Take off your clothes and join us. We could have an orgy like the one we had in college, but this time you can be the boss," he said.

"She will do anything I say?" Angela asked.

"Yes, give her a command and try her out," he said.

Angela walked over to the clone and whispered something in the clone's ear. The clone smiled at her. Angela began to take off her clothes while the cloned went to her husband.

"Fuck me, baby," the clone said to Blanco.

"No problem," he said, smiling, as he let her guide him to the floor. He watched as she mounted him and took his cock deep inside her.

Angela eased to her knees and began to play with the clone's large breasts. Something told her that the agent's breasts were not quite so large. She had seen A1 and the improvements Blanco had made to her clone for Asmodais. Too bad he had not made her a dyke too.

"Damn, I am about to go off," Blanco moaned.

He never saw the blow coming. The clone popped his neck with one quick, solid karate chop.

"Good girl. He died a happy man. You did great. I told you to fuck him to death. You did a wonderful job," Angela told the clone.

"Yes, ma'am, I am glad to be of service to you. I was made to be controlled by a female, not a male," the clone said calmly.

"Can you be a dyke?" Angela asked.

"Yes, ma'am, I can be a very good dyke," the clone responded.

"Good, let's go to my bedroom. I need you to treat me rough tonight."

Al Tells All

Asmodais Winters arrived back at the compound from the retreat around two-thirty in the morning. He had spent the last three hours visiting women in the Stamford area. He had gone to a party arranged by one of the older women he had done in the limo on Sunday. He had impregnated over seven women in the three-hour span. Because of those women, the five young nuns, and Mother Superior, he needed relief, and he knew exactly where to come to get that relief. However, he was back on schedule with his quota for Iblis.

He went to his bedroom and smiled when he saw the Al on his bed where he had left her some two days earlier. She was still wearing the number one he had tattooed on her right breast. He had told her that he wanted to make sure that he was doing the right one. Later he would have a number tattooed on each of the female clones. The other human staff members had been impregnated and sent on their way, except for the German woman who had been burned to a crisp by his neglect. In a few days the human staff would be replenished.

"Are you in rest mode?" he asked.

"The command to go into rest mode was sent out twice while you were away, but my command did not take effect," she said.

"Why didn't it take effect?"

"A1 has an overriding command to sense out danger to the master and to the compound."

"What danger was there to me?" he asked.

"Two nights ago the scientist who made me returned to correct a problem with his experiment. He was not alone. He was with a woman, the FBI agent," she reported.

"It was FBI Agent Samantha Lee?" Asmodais attempted to stay calm.

"Yes, Master, I turned on the surveillance system for the internal building while the intruders were on site. I summoned the guards, but they were all in sleep mode," A1 said.

"You said *intruders*. That means more than one intruder," Asmodais prompted her.

"Yes, the man who had been with the agent earlier that day had been hiding in the trunk of the vehicle. He followed them to the basement and hid while the scientist cloned the FBI agent. He returned to the vehicle before the others returned to the garage. The three of them were able to leave the grounds unnoticed by the guards. Then tonight Blanco placed the security guards in rest mode and left with two female clones," A1 reported.

"Two clones? He made two clones of the FBI agent?" Asmodais was getting more irritated.

"There were two clones made of the woman," she said.

"How is the experiment going in the lab?" he asked.

"The clone of the scientist was recently completed, but it failed. The clone turned itself off permanently. The scientist did not return last night or this morning. The clone cannot function without an injection immediately after it has been made. The injection was not forthcoming," she said.

"Are you ready to replace your original?" he asked.

"Yes, master, all my programming has been completed," A1 responded.

"When she arrives this morning, see to it. Either kill her or have one of the guards do it," he ordered.

"I can handle the task if my master wishes it to be so," she said.

"I do," he said. "When I return from the retreat this afternoon, I want her to be gone. If her husband is not gone, I want him dead also."

"It will be done, Master," she said.

"This is very frustrating. I cannot believe that Marsala was this close to me," he said furiously. Thanks to the bishop, that problem had been eliminated. The bishop had called him yesterday morning with the good news. He no longer worried about the VEF agent.

"Sir, if you require a body to vent your anger on, my body is at your disposal," A1 said.

"Your body is not required. Send me another clone of your original, and I will vent my anger on that body," he said.

"A2 is on her way." The elevator opened immediately, and a second version of Angela appeared.

Asmodais destroyed the second clone in a matter of seconds, ripping the body to shreds. Another image appeared, and he destroyed that image too. By the time his anger had subsided, A1 was the only clone left.

He needed to make plans for the FBI agent to visit Winterhaven. She would never leave the complex alive. He would do to her what he had done to the German woman but more slowly. He would allow her to enjoy being impregnated; then he would burn her and his seed to a crisp.

When he had finally vented his anger, he took A1 into his bedroom and enjoyed her.

Plan A

Jenny Lynn had gone through three of the four steps toward changing her body into a protective heat shield, but the test heat was still too much for her body. She had been able to last the heat out for thirty-two minutes. However, she had to be able to maintain the heat for exactly forty-five minutes.

Meanwhile the android Jane had adjusted her body to accept the fluids and an egg from a donor. It was now a matter of testing the fluids. The two of them generated the acceptable levels of heat required and noted that the fluid had maintained the desired temperature. The egg would not be implanted until the last minute.

Jane suggested they use the egg sent over from Paris recently instead of using Jenny's current egg. Jenny finally agreed with her. It was a simple test. If it worked, then Jenny would have another egg ready very soon. If both plans worked, then Jenny could have two eggs in her at the same time and possibly conceive twin sons.

Asmodais returned to the retreat shortly after eight in the morning. Jenny could see that he was upset about something, but she had to do this plan A test now.

"Master, Jane and I would like to run another test this morning," she said as they both ate breakfast.

"I am busy today. I don't have time for your tests," he said abruptly.

"Then perhaps you do not want a male offspring at all," she said very calmly.

"This is just not the time. I am too busy." Asmodais looked annoyed.

"Then fuck you too. Enjoy producing female offspring only and never having a son by me," she said and stomped out of the kitchen.

She ran to the master bedroom and jumped onto the bed. She pretended to cry. She knew he would follow her. And he did.

"Okay, what is this test?" he asked, sitting down on the bed next to her.

"What do you care? You are too busy to care," she repined, face still in the pillow.

"Honey, two nights ago an FBI agent and the man from the Vatican Elite Force were able to break into Winterhaven. I have to make sure that doesn't happen again." Asmodais put one strong hand on her rear and stroked her.

"That is not it at all. You have created more clones at the lab, and they are enjoying the real you. You don't need me anymore." Jenny raised her tearful face to him. She had long ago learned to cry real tears to get what she wanted.

"Honey, I could create a thousand clones, and all of them combined wouldn't be half as good as you are."

"What good am I to you? I can't give you everything you want. Jane and I have been working on two plans. We have implanted an egg and some of my fluids inside her cooling system. We have set up a timing mechanism so that at the end of five hours, my fluids will ease into her collector to encourage the sperm to feed. Then, in twenty-seven minutes, the egg will appear, and the sperm can join to the egg. Twenty hours later we can transfer the fertilized egg back inside me and let it grow naturally," she explained.

"What is plan two?" he asked.

"I have been undergoing heat treatment. I can maintain your heat for over thirty minutes. One more session, and I hope to reach forty-five minutes. We have solved the brain problem by implanting stereo music to filter into the brain cells from the beginning until the end. As long as we get no interruptions, we should be able to enjoy ourselves to the fullest," she said.

"So what do you need me to do?" he asked.

"Nothing right now! You are too busy!" Jenny pretended to pout.

"Come on, let's go downstairs and see Jane!" Asmodais rose and pulled her to her feet.

"No, you are too busy!" Jenny kept up her pretense a little longer.

"Come on!" Asmodais swatted her gently on the bottom.

Together the two of them went down to the lab. Jane was waiting for them. She explained the procedure to Asmodais again. Jenny stepped behind the wall and waited for the hot light to begin. She came around and watched for as long as she could before darting back behind the wall.

Forty-five minutes later, she saw the light dim. As she came around the corner, she saw the smiling face of Jane.

"I think it worked. We won't know for sure for twenty hours," Jane said.

"Can we do my last treatment now?" Jenny asked as Asmodais dressed.

"Yes, we have time." Jane said.

"Ladies, I have to go tend to some business," Asmodais told them. He still had quotas to be met.

"Thank you!" Jenny gave him a big hug and a very French kiss.

Marsala Gets Another Ally

Angela Blanco awoke beside the clone. The night with the clone had been all she expected and more. Her husband had done well in creating this model. She wondered if the original model could have been such a dyke. Marvin could not make a clone out of thin air. Sure he could add physical traits to the clone, but the mental capacity had to come directly from the original.

She considered the ramifications if Asmodais learned of the existence of this clone. She could attempt to convince him that she knew nothing about the clone until she came home that night. It was the truth, but would he believe her? She knew she should have reported the clone to Asmodais immediately.

"A1 is searching for original," the clone said, staring at the ceiling.

Angela then remembered that all the clones had the ability to communicate with each other. It was a program Asmodais had insisted upon from the beginning. A1 was her initial clone. Was it that A1 was looking for her, or was Asmodais looking for her?

"Why is A1 looking for me?" Angela asked.

"A1's master has requested elimination of A1's original," the clone responded.

"Will you kill me?" Angela asked softly.

"My connection to A1's master has not been completed. Mistress Angela is only master relationship that has been connected. Cannot sever relationship with current master at this time," the clone responded.

Angela breathed a sigh of relief. At least she had a little time on her side. However, to survive, she needed to create a plan and carry it out quickly.

"Would my master wish me to continue in mode of last orders?" the clone asked.

Angela smiled to herself. The clone was still in a domineering dyke mode, the way she had been most of the night, at least until Angela put her in rest mode to regenerate.

She named her S1 and placed the clone into passive mode for the time being until she had the answers she needed It was then that she learned that Blanco had lied to her and made two clones and that the FBI agent had her own copy of S1. Fortunately there had only been two clones made, and no more could be created without the original. She also discovered that the two FBI agent clones could communicate with each other, but currently the other clone was in rest mode.

"S2 has been placed in rest mode and has turned off the ability to track her presence," S1 said.

"Can you turn off tracking too?" Angela asked.

"It has been done," S1 said.

Angela needed to know if the clone could track the original—not only the original of S1, but the possibility that A1 could track her too. S1 gave her the address where her original was at the moment.

Angela thought for a few seconds. If S1 could track her original, then surely A1 could track her original too. "Is A1 coming after me?" she asked.

"Clones cannot travel alone without specific directions. They must be controlled by a master. A1 is aware of original location only when original is in stationary position for more than one minute," S1 said.

"Then we have to keep on the move until I devise a plan that will save us both. I need to take a shower, then we must leave," Angela said, rising from the bed.

S1, perched on the edge of the bed, offered yet more information. "Water is another disconnection with other clones."

"Explain," Angela said. Despite the situation, she found herself staring at the beautiful body.

"There are three times when clones are out of reach of other clones. First is when clone is in travel mode, second is when in water, and third when sex is involved. Travel scatters the location counter, water provides a filter that cannot be passed by clone senses, and sex causes all the senses to be dedicated to the task at hand so that no outside communication is possible," S1 explained.

"So ... whenever I don't want a clone to find me, I can use one of those three methods, and the other clones cannot find me?"

"Yes, that is a true fact about clones," S1 confirmed.

"Where is A1 at this time?" Angela asked.

"A1 is at rest at the compound," S1 said rising from the bed.

"Come on, then, we must take a shower," Angela ordered.

"Yes, master," S1 said, rising from the bed.

"You can call me Angela, and I will call you S1," Angela said, smiling more widely and more friendly.

"Then Angela does not like the names used last night?" S1 asked innocently.

"Those names are fine when you are in a domineering mode, but in a subservient mode, *Angela* will do fine. While we are in the shower, by the way, you can resume the domineering mode," Angela said as she led the clone to the bathroom.

S1 did her best to comply. "Yes, you pussy-licking bitch, let's take a shower."

Angela laughed as the two of them stepped into the shower area.

Thirty minutes later, when the clone had returned to submissive mode, Angela led S1 to the car. They sped away.

Twenty one minutes later she pulled into the Ridgefield Inn.

"The original is on the first floor in the back. Room 198," S1 said.

Angela parked near the room. "Come with me," she ordered, and the two of them got out of the car.

She knocked softly on the door. Marsala opened the door and leveled his Luger at Angela.

"Don't shoot. I need your help. We need each other's help," Angela said quickly.

He stepped back, and she entered with S1. She spotted Samantha Lee sitting on the bed wearing a long, oversized tee shirt that covered everything but concealed very little. The tee shirt obviously belonged to Marsala. She could tell the parts that Blanco had improved upon.

"S1, go take a shower," Angela ordered.

"What is going on?" Marsala asked.

"Clones can be tracked only when they are not in traveling, in water, or having sex. S1, do as I told you to do," Angela ordered.

S1 left them and went to the bathroom. Soon the water was running.

"Why are you here?" Marsala asked, still keeping the pistol aimed at Angela.

"Last night when I came home, I found Marvin in the garage with one of your clones. He tried to 'explain everything.' Unfortunately for him, I ordered S1 to kill him ... I had no choice. I couldn't return her to the compound, so I kept her last night. All the clones are genetically linked, so S1 informed me this morning that Asmodais has ordered my clone, A1, to eliminate me. She has a link to me, as S1 has to you. A1 probably knows where I am, so we will have to move very soon. She has a link to S1 also. That is why she is in the shower," Angela said.

"So Asmodais wants to kill you too? Welcome to the club." Marsala kept the gun trained on her.

"I don't know where you have S2," Angela told Samantha Lee, "but you should mentally tell her to get into a shower and remain there for a while."

"How do I do that?" Samantha asked.

"Just think it, and the order will be given," Angela said.

"Done," Samantha said, smiling from the bed.

"How do we know this is not a trick devised by Asmodais?" Marsala asked.

"You don't know. I can only assure you that I am on his hit list too, but I do have a plan," Angela said.

"What plan?" Marsala still wasn't convinced she was being entirely truthful.

"We need to blow up Asmodais's one source of income in America—Winterhaven," Angela responded.

"That is easier said than done. Winterhaven security is very tight," Marsala said. But he knew she already knew that fact.

"Yes, but it is not impossible. We cannot kill Asmodais, but we can get him to flee from America back to his compound in France," Angela said.

"My mission is to kill him," Marsala said.

"Yes, I know of your mission and your connection to the Vatican Elite Force, and so does Asmodais. I must admit I think he fears you more than any of your other peers because he does not believe he is on safe ground here in America." Angela spoke more calmly now that he had lowered his weapon and the gun was not pointed at her heart anymore.

"How do we blow up the compound?" Marsala asked.

"I am sure that Marvin gave you a switch to turn off the guards, didn't he?" Angela said to Samantha Lee.

"Yes, but that does not turn off the security measures," Samantha said.

"Hey, you pussy-eating bitch, come here," S1 called from the shower.

Angela laughed. "She must have inadvertently turned herself back to dyke mode in the shower. Hey in there, you're strictly sub now!" she called to the clone.

"She has a dyke mode?" Samantha sounded amused.

"You can take the credit. She got that from you. Marvin could never have created that in her," Angela told her.

"Okay, back to the problem at hand," Marsala said sternly. He did not appear to be amused that Samantha's clone had a dyke mode.

"I am expected to return to the compound. I can get inside and turn off the external security monitor. The two of you could enter and go to the basement and press a few computer switches and set the systems to destruct mode. The self-destruct program is already in place. All you have to do is execute the program," Angela said.

"When?" Marsala asked.

"We should do it this afternoon. Asmodais always goes to the retreat in the afternoon for three hours. He will not be on site, so if we all work quickly, the job could be done in less than an hour," Angela said.

"Won't that kill a lot of people?" Samantha asked.

"There are no people working at Winterhaven. Everything has been automated and is run by clones. The females who lived there are all gone at the moment. There is only one clone that could possibly cause a problem, and that is A1. Of course there are ten of her, but if I can control one of them, I can control all of them. A1 is the key. She is the only one with an implanted program to defend the compound and to protect her master," Angela said.

"But aren't you her master?" Samantha asked.

"No, Asmodais is her master, just as he was my master. By now he would have solidified that relationship. A1 will not be so easy to get by, but the one thing in our favor is that she does not have control over the other clones, not yet anyway. Given time, I am certain Asmodais would program her to be the absolute security at Winterhaven. That is the reason we have to act quickly," Angela said.

"Okay, we have no choice but to do this. Let's make it happen," Marsala said, lowering the gun completely.

"I must go over a few of the security measures in case something does go wrong. We can do that on the way," Angela said.

"What of her?" Samantha asked.

"She will be fine until we get back. Let me give her a couple of orders while you dress," Angela said, smiling as she walked to the bathroom door.

Samantha arose from the bed and started to dress quickly.

"S1, you will remain in the shower until the cleaning person gets here. If it is a female, go into dyke mode. If it is a man, go into submissive mode. If no one comes within an hour, I want you to dress and run back to my apartment. Yes, it is twenty-five miles, but I want you to keep up a steady pace. If I am not there when you get there, go to the house next door. You'll find a man who lives alone. He will know exactly what to do with you. Make sure the sex lasts a very long time," Angela ordered then returned to the other two, who were already dressed.

"I'm not so sure I like the idea of your clone fucking everything in sight," Samantha reflected.

"It is what she does best, and it will keep the other clones from tracking her. Do you have a better idea?" Angela said.

"Actually, I do," Samantha said opening her cell phone. She pressed a speed dial number.

The other eyes were on her.

"Leroy, I am at the Ridgeway Inn, and I'm very lonely. Can you come by and visit me? The door will be unlocked, so come on in. I will be in the shower. I am in Room 198. Bring that little cheerleader outfit for me. You know the one I like. Can't wait to see you," Samantha said, smiling as she hung up. "Tell S1 to pretend to be totally me and give Leroy a fabulous time!"

While Angela was giving the orders to S1, Marsala just shook his head and smiled ruefully.

Samantha noticed his expression. "Well, that is better than having her running from here to Stamford. That would look weird enough to attract some attention nobody here needs. Besides, wouldn't you rather the clone be enjoying Leroy rather than me? I know how jealous you are."

The three of them left the Ridgefield Inn in two cars. Marsala parked his in a car dealership lot amidst other vehicles that looked like it near the Winterhaven compound, and the three entered the compound in Angela's car.

Plan A Fails. On with Plan B!

Jenny Lynn checked on Jane every two hours that morning. Everything was looking perfect until almost noon, immediately after Jane had completed the final treatment on Jenny. Asmodais had left but promised to return by noon. He said something about keeping up his quota. She didn't know what that meant, but how could she argue with him? She couldn't.

"Plan A has failed," Jane said to Jenny as she re-entered the lab area.

Jenny stared at the android. She knew there was something wrong. Jane had changed her skin tone from her normal tone to a suntanned dark brown. "What is wrong?" Jenny asked.

"The fluids mingled with coolant properly, but as the coolant and fluids were being dispersed into my system, a small pore was opened. The heat seeped through and burned out several critical functions. It has taken six hours to determine the final results. I have been fatally damaged. I have spent the last hour downloading all my data into the computer. The master will have to make another model of me for the future," Jane told her.

"How long do you have?" Jenny asked.

"I am in shutdown mode now. I was hoping I could survive long enough to transfer the egg to you, but the egg has been destroyed. The plan failed. The data will explain what to do the next time if I have time to download it all." Jane then shut down completely.

Jenny screamed, "No, Jane, you android bitch, you can't fail me now. I need all your fucking data. The master needs the damn data. You can't shut down until the download has completed. Turn back on, bitch!"

But Jane made to motion to obey the teenage woman. She stood there with a blank look on her face.

It took Jenny the better part of five minutes to calm down, but she knew there was a backup plan. She had to be calm to execute the second plan.

Jenny knew the download had not completed. Plan A had failed; now her only option was Plan B. She had twenty minutes to prepare herself before Asmodais, her father, would arrive for the afternoon session. She needed to be totally committed to making this happen. She double-checked everything. The stereo set was ready to cover her brain. She had the music set to ninety minutes. Yes, it was longer than forty-five minutes, but she needed to make sure. Asmodais had only been in one woman who had survived the experience, and she had survived it as some kind of human turnip, in a life support ward, with a tube up her nose. Would it take him longer than with Jane? Double the time would be better for both of them.

She tested a torch against her skin. She did not burn. She stepped into the alloy shower. She needed to make sure all external pores were closed. There must be no way the heat could get inside her body at the wrong places. She wondered if she was more jinn than human if she was then she would survive this ordeal.

"Plan A failed," a male voice called to her as she stepped out of the shower.

"Yes, Jane was able to download a portion of the data, but I don't think she got all of it," she said.

"So you are determined to go on with Plan B."

She climbed into the chair. "Yes, I am prepared for Plan B."

"And if it kills you?" he said.

"Then you can create another like me and try again in the future," she said smiling up at him.

"There will never be another one like you," he said as the room became pitch black.

Jenny felt his heat begin to rise once he was inside her. It did not seem as hot as she seemed to recall, but he'd only just begun. There were still at least forty-five minutes to go.

At the twenty-minute mark she was still holding her own as she was at the thirty-minute mark. She thought of the long hard rides on Smoke and how tiring those rides had been but she had endured those rides. She was happy when they passed the forty-minute mark. They were coming down the home-stretch now. All she had to do was hang on through the finish line. How many orgasms had she had by that point? Had her fluids all burned away? Had her egg been destroyed? She didn't think so.

Then at forty-two minutes, she felt a burning sensation. It burned, really burned! She was in untested territory. Not only was the heat almost unbearable—so was the pounding inside her womb. She was surprised when she had another orgasm and the fluids from the orgasm calmed the burning and eased the pounding. She could now see the finish line. She could see the last hurdle. If Smoke could pass that hurdle, then so could she. She was ready. She had ridden the race of her life.

At exactly forty-five minutes, she felt the explosion inside her. His explosion caused her to have a giant orgasm at exactly the same time. She latched onto him as hard as she could; she hoped to keep him inside her long enough for the sperm to reach her egg.

As the heat lessened, she found it easier to hold onto his body. At the fifty-minute mark, she had his body totally under her control, squeezing him with her long legs high around his waist. After exactly an hour, he eased out of her, and his external heat had subsided. The internal heat remained, but it was not nearly as intense as it had been.

He smiled down at her, separated her thighs, bent over her, and gave her a long wet kiss.

"I survived!"

"Yes, that was wonderful," he said, smiling.

"Was it as good you've had with Jane?" she asked.

"A clone or an android are convenient, but you ...mostly jinn and partly human, beautiful, underage, wanton, willing, and my daughter ... a million forbidden pleasures at once."

"I hope your sperm found a receptive egg," she said softly.

"Whether you are pregnant this time or not, the fact that I now have a human body to share my ultimate pleasure with is the best news I could have hoped for."

"You can have this body anytime you want it."

"We will know within six hours if the child inside of you is alive," he said.

"I thought we had to wait twenty-four hours!"

"The woman that almost bore my son before was well developed after six hours. We will know the truth in the same amount of time."

"Go take care of Mother. I have a few things I must do alone, things that Jane and I discussed," Jenny said smiling at him.

He left her, and she stepped back into the alloy shower to repair any residual damage.

Later she went up to the main area. Her mother was smiling. She knew her father had taken care of her mother.

Winterhaven

A1 received the signal to go into rest mode along with all the other clones at the compound, but another program overrode her rest mode program. Asmodais had reprogrammed her to go to rest on his own command only. She watched as all the other clones returned to their quarters. Something was not right. It was just after noon; there was no reason to go into a rest period.

She stared at the security monitor and recognized the automobile entering the compound and the underground garage. It carried her original and two other people. Why were they in the compound, and why had her original placed the clones in sleep mode? No, there was definitely something wrong.

She attempted to contact Asmodais, but he could not be reached. She had no choice but to take matters into her own hands and protect the compound.

She watched the monitor as her original took the elevator up to the second level; then the other two rode the elevator to the bottom level. When the two reached the bottom level, she sealed the elevator. They were now trapped underground. She could have sent out the intruder alert, but how would she be able to prove her worth to the master if the security clones were involved? She could handle this emergency alone. This should be easy.

Angela Blanco entered the quarters of Asmodais. She knew he wouldn't be there, but she also knew this was the only place that she would find A1 if the clone had not gone into rest mode. She saw the clone standing at Asmodais's large desk as she entered the room. She also noted the body parts of the other clones stacked in the corner. Obviously Asmodais had been quite upset with someone or something and taken it out on her clones. She quickly switched A1 into the OFF mode.

"Only the master can turn me off," A1 reported stoically.

"So it would seem," Angela said, disappointed that she had been unable to shut off A1 immediately.

"The master is very upset with you. You have betrayed him," A1 remarked. She did not move from behind the desk. She was still monitoring the progress of the two in the computer room. "Your friends will never make it out of the computer room," A1 told Angela.

"That is very possible, but they don't need to make it out to complete their plan," Angela said calmly.

"They do not appear to be ready to die. They will not detonate the computer facility without an escape route. I have shut off the elevator," A1 said.

"So you are now my replacement. I find it hard to believe that a clone can perform as well as a human," Angela said, smiling. She had to buy time for the others to complete their mission.

"I am capable of doing any service that you can perform for the master and doing it better," A1 retorted.

"I don't think so. Your physical attributes may be stronger, but can you reproduce for him? You see, all you are is a fucking machine. He can create a dozen more like you and better than you. But what you can't do is provide a lineage for him," Angela said.

"Neither can you. You are barren," A1 said without hesitation.

"Yes, that is true, but I can be implanted with an egg, and I can reproduce for him. So, you see, I still am better than you are." Angela provided her own version of the truth.

"My body will never age. The master can use me forever. You would grow old and die," A1 said.

"Yes, but I can feel him inside of me. I am not merely a box for him to use when he wants to get his jollies off. All you can do is let him enjoy your body; you can't enjoy him. That is why a clone will never replace a human even in sexual relationships," Angela said. She recalled, though, that Marvin had made S1 very sensitive sexually. Had he done the same for A1? She didn't think so.

"You are buying time for your comrades, but it won't work. I will kill them too," A1 said.

"I don't think so," Angela said calmly as she raised the German Luger she had borrowed from Marsala and put a bullet between the clone's eyes.

A1 stood motionlessly for a few seconds, then she pressed a key on the computer and dropped to the floor.

"Rest period over—intruder alert!" started blaring all over the building.

Angela ran to the elevator that connected Asmodais's office to the computer room. She only had a few seconds to reach Marsala and Samantha Lee before the guard clones would be looking for a way into the computer room. Time was of the essence.

The elevator opened on the bottom level. She spotted Marsala immediately.

"A1 alerted the guards. We must leave," she called out to them.

"Put them back in rest mode," Marsala yelled.

"I can't do that until the intruder alert has been satisfied. They will not stop until they have found the intruder. We will be safe for a few minutes in Asmodais's office. It is the only place," Angela called out.

The three of them jumped into the elevator and were up in the office area quickly. Angela went to the monitor. "Good, they are having problems. The elevator to the basement has been locked. It will take them a few minutes to find another route to the computer room. Unfortunately the only other route is through this office. Here, help me hide A1. We can stack her with the other clone bodies. I have a plan!"

"Is she dead?" Samantha asked.

"The only way to kill them for sure is a bullet between the eyes. It affects their brain and shuts them down immediately—well, almost immediately. Is everything completed in the computer room?" Angela asked.

"Yes, we did everything you told us to do," Marsala reported.

"Good, hide in the far corner behind the metal curtain," she ordered.

The couple moved quickly.

Angela activated the PA system and spoke in A1's normal tones. "This is A1. All security personnel report to the second floor office. The intruders are trapped in the computer facility. They can be reached via the elevator in the master's office." She released the elevator from the computer room floor and programmed it to travel upward only. She watched as the security clones got into the elevator.

Almost immediately, twelve security officers entered the office area.

"A1 has killed the original. The original was with the intruding humans. These humans are dangerous. Take the internal elevator and eradicate them," Angela ordered.

Without hesitation, the twelve guards pushed their way into the nearby elevator. The door closed, and she watched the light on the computer room indicator turn yellow. They were there. She immediately shut down the elevator. The security guards were now trapped in the elevator.

"We don't have much time. We must hurry," she said, unlocking the garage area from the console on Asmodais's desk.

The three of them rushed out of the room and hurried to the basement. She drove through the garage gate just before it closed. They barely made it out before the second gate closed behind them.

"How did they do that?' Marsala asked.

"They didn't. I placed the security gates on delayed lockdown as soon as we left just in case someone decided to follow us," Angela said.

Behind them was a loud explosion.

Angela drove to a parking place that overlooked the complex below. They all watched as the entire building collapsed in a matter of minutes.

Marsala stared at the rubble. "It is too bad Asmodais was not in the building."

"If Asmodais had been there, none of this could have happened. He would have destroyed us the moment we entered the compound," Angela said, perhaps with regret. Asmodais was still her master, and with A1 gone, he would have turned to her again.

"Where is he?" Samantha asked.

"He has a retreat in the mountains. I have been there a few times but only by his automated helicopter. As far as I know, there is no way to get there by car or on foot. The valley has slick walls over a hundred feet high and laden with booby traps all along the way," Angela said.

"I know that valley. A friend of mine and I went camping there," Samantha said.

Marsala glanced at her and shook his head.

"Yes, he was a good friend at the time. Don't get jealous," Samantha joked.

"You said the only way to get to the retreat was by helicopter, right?" Marsala asked.

"Yes, the side of the cliff opens, and the landing base is inside the cavern," Angela responded. "There are sensors all over the valley. They are usually turned on when he is there."

"How close can you get us?" Marsala asked Samantha.

"I can get us close enough for government work," Samantha responded.

"We should go pick up my clone," Angela said starting the car.

"Why do we need her?" Marsala asked.

"She has strength that might be very valuable to us. If anyone can get us by the valley security, she could," Angela said.

"Would two clones be better than one?" Samantha asked.

"Possibly," Angela said. This had not been part of her plan. She had hoped that her clone would warn Asmodais and he would be ready for them. If she could help him destroy the agents, then he would turn to her.

"Okay, drop us off at my car, and we'll meet you at the motel in thirty minutes," Marsala said.

Angela dropped them off and sped away.

Once they were alone, Samantha suggested that they stop by the FBI arsenal to pick up some hardware. She said the arsenal agent owed her a couple of favors. Marsala had learned not to ask her what she had done to put people in her debt.

The woman at the arsenal was very friendly toward Samantha and helped her load two bazookas and enough shells and grenades to blow up a mountain. The way the two women hugged and kissed before they left the area amused Marsala, but he said nothing. They stopped by the nunnery and picked up her clone. Angela was waiting with S1 when they reached the motel, and they headed toward the mountains immediately. No one asked the clone what had happened to Leroy, but the clone was still wearing a very suggestive cheerleading outfit.

Asmodais Reacts to the Explosion

When Asmodais exited the shower with Jenny, he shuddered.

"I felt it too," Jenny said, toweling off.

"The bastards blew up Winterhaven! Years of research have been destroyed. This is twice that someone in America has gotten close to me," he said angrily.

"We are safe here, aren't we?" Jenny asked.

"This is the safest place in America, but this area might not be enough. I sense they will come here. I have no doubt about that," he said. He knew he could completely disappear if he needed to, but that would not save the women. Nor would it save the first son he had sired on a human woman.

"What can I do to help?" she asked.

"If my experience is right, Angela Blanco is helping them. I am no longer in contact with A1, so I must assume the clone failed in her mission to destroy her original. However, they may be making a mistake," he said.

"What mistake?" Jenny asked.

"They will undoubtedly try to use the two clones to assist them. What they don't realize is that all clones are attached to me subconsciously. When they are near, the clones will inform me of their presence. I do not feel that Angela Blanco will desert me so readily," he said.

Jenny felt reassured. "I still feel good inside."

"Good. We should know the results in a few more hours. My hope is that you are with child, my child." Asmodais brushed the long strands of red hair from her face.

"That is my hope too," she said, smiling up at him.

"Come, I wish to show you and your mother a place to hide in the event things get out of hand," he said as they dressed.

He led both mother and daughter to the rear of the main cave and down to the lab area and into a separate portal. He led them quickly into a very dark area. A light appeared, showing stairs leading upward. As they ascended the stairs, the area behind them closed as if there had never been a door in the stone. After climbing almost one hundred feet, they entered another cavern that housed a full apartment. He had never used this space, but it was even more secure than the main cave below.

"You will be comfortable here for quite a long while," he said.

"This is beautiful," Alice said, softly running her hands along the slick walls.

"Stay here for now. I will be back later or I will send someone to get you," Asmodais said as he left by the route he had used to bring them here.

"Mother, I may be having a son!" Jenny said to her mother.

"I know. He told me after your session this afternoon. I can hardly wait for the positive results!" Alice hugged her daughter.

Asmodais returned to the main entry cavern. He reviewed all the monitors in the valley. He was convinced they had not reached the valley yet, but he knew they would be there soon. He could not believe that A1 had allowed the compound to be destroyed. She had failed him. Would Angela fail him too?

He tried to contact the Lee clones but was unable to do so. Had Blanco figured a way to counter his programming? He didn't believe that Blanco was that intelligent, but the man had fooled him before. Had A1 not alerted him about the clones, he might never have known about them. Blanco must have discovered a way to cover their presence. He would have to capture one of them and dissect the brain if he could.

Had Marsala survived the onslaught of the bishop? The bishop had called him and told him that Marsala had been killed last night. But this morning, while he was fulfilling his quota, one of the women he visited had mentioned the death of the bishop in his confessional booth. The only person in America that would dare kill a bishop had to be a member of the VEF, like Marsala. Perhaps Marsala had been more resourceful than he had anticipated. Perhaps it was better to give Marsala one hint of victory. If he hurried, his plan might just work. He almost ran to the lab and opened the hidden storeroom in the rear. He found what he was looking for. It was an android of him. Not a real clone, but a very good likeness. He told the robot to follow him and led him up to the main chamber. He had made it just in time. One of the alarms went off and then was silenced. The clones were being used. He knew that for sure now. He could feel them across the valley on a ridge. But he couldn't communicate with them. What had Blanco done to keep this communication one-sided and to the clones' advantage?

The Retreat Is Destroyed

Marsala looked across the valley at the steep, almost glasslike cliffs.

"The entrance is about two thirds of the way up the cliff face," Angela said, pointing in the direction of the cliff. She still did not believe they could manage to destroy the cave.

Marsala raised a bazooka and scanned the cliff. There was no perceptible spot for an opening. He hadn't expected there would be.

"The clones are ready," Samantha Lee called to him. She was about twenty feet away from him and staring through a bazooka's sight at the cliff too.

"Go for it," Marsala called to the clones.

The two clones threw hand grenades simultaneously toward the cliff. They were a lot stronger than their originals. The grenades exploded on the cliff about two-thirds of the way up the face. Not only did the grenades explode, but so did two countermeasures embedded in the face of the cliff.

"That should shake up things a bit," Marsala said as he maintained a visual inspection of the cliff face through the scope on the bazooka. He knew that Samantha Lee was trained on the same area with her bazooka.

An opening in the cliff face appeared out of seemingly nowhere, and the sound of the helicopter could be heard. As planned, as soon as the opening was large enough, two more grenades were tossed by the clones into the area, and Samantha shot her bazooka round into the same opening. He could see the explosions erupt from the inside. Samantha dropped another round into the now opened cave like the markswoman she was. He waited. His target had not yet appeared.

Then he saw the nose of the helicopter as it emerged at the entrance. He knew he only had one shot. He waited until he could see the entire helicopter, then he sent his bazooka round barreling toward the target. He saw the stoic face of Asmodais staring at him. Then the helicopter exploded and tumbled down the face of the cliff, burning as it dropped. When it hit the bottom, the chopper exploded into a ball of fire. He shot two more rounds into the debris, and more explosions followed.

Samantha laughed. "I'd say that was overkill!"

"Was it overkill?" Marsala was about to pump another round into the fire below.

"He is still in there," one of the clones almost shouted.

"Then let's seal him in for eternity," Marsala yelled. "Blow the fucking mountain up!"

"I don't believe a priest should use that word," Samantha laughed as she shot round after round into the cave.

The clones were busy detonating other parts of the cliff face with their grenades.

Angela Blanco could only watch. She had no skills that would have helped Asmodais in this battle. Her clone was doing very well, and that was all that mattered. She watched as the cave fell. She felt a little remorseful that the man she had called her master was now trapped inside that cave. Obviously Asmodais had used a clone or an android to pilot the helicopter.

Thirty minutes later the last round was fired. The mountain area around the cave appeared to have dropped at least ten feet.

"We do not feel his presence," one of the clones reported.

"Does that mean he is dead?" Angela asked. She had a hard time believing Asmodais was dead. She did not want to be convinced he was dead.

"Do not know the answer to the question, only that Asmodais's presence cannot be detected," the clone responded.

"Nothing could have lived through that barrage, but if you like, we can go and verify. It might take a month to dig it out," Samantha said, lowering her bazooka.

"I am satisfied if the clones are satisfied," Marsala said, staring at the crushed opening in the face of the mountain.

"Then we are done," Samantha said.

"Yes," he said.

"What do we do with them?" Samantha asked, pointing to the clones.

He put his weapon aside. "That is your problem, not mine."

Samantha put a bullet between the eyes of S1 and watched the clone as it fell over the cliff and into the fire below. "Sorry, Angela, I know that you would have preferred to keep S1, but this is my reputation we are discussing here. I can't have the entire population of Connecticut thinking that FBI agents are always as easy as S1."

"I understand," Angela said, staring into the fire. Was Asmodais really dead?

"Angela, I too am sorry for what must be done," Marsala said pulling out his Luger. "Asmodais has corrupted you more than other women. You have been his ally for too many years. I have no choice about this."

Angela moved toward the edge of the cliff. She knew Marsala was right and that she had to die. If Asmodais was dead, then she had no reason to live. She leaped over the edge of the cliff and into the burning furnace.

Samantha gave him a long, hard look. "I am glad she came to that decision alone."

"Yes, it was the right decision on her part," he said, putting his Luger away.

He turned and looked at S2. "What do we do with this one?" he asked Samantha.

"I can control her. She will enhance my reputation. I know you don't think I have a good reputation, but I think I do," Samantha said, moving to the clone. "I think I will call her Sam."

"You actually have a good reputation. It has been a pleasure working with you on this assignment," Marsala said, sounding cool and calm again. They went back to the car.

Asmodais Dies?

During the flurry of bombing and walls falling, Asmodais had made it up to the comfort of the cave where the two women were waiting for him. He could see them huddled together, holding each other. They ran to him.

"We thought they killed you!"

"I am not so easy to kill as all that. I have withstood a lot more than they threw at me today and survived. My thoughts now are for your safety."

"What happens now?" Jenny asked stopping near him.

He moved his hand to her stomach and rubbed her gently. "The child lived through all of this."

"Your son is very strong."

"Unfortunately, in order to save you, I must leave now. As long as the clones can detect my presence in the caves, the bombing will not end. I must get back to the safety of my Paris compound," he said, looking Jenny in the eyes.

"What will happen to us?" Jenny said, caressing his hand on her belly.

"In a few hours, I will send someone to pick you up and carry you back to the Lynn Estate. You will be safe there, for the time being, until I can send for you. It will be for a short period only then we will be together as a family. I would take you with me if I could, but your safety and the safety of my son is most important. Wait a few hours after I have left. After the bombing has ended, go to the back of the cave. Someone will come and rescue you. Now do as I say. Perhaps we can fool the Vatican Elite Force long enough for you to survive this ordeal."

"We will be together again?" Jenny asked.

"Do not worry. I will take care of you and your mother. You will never want for anything. And when our son is old enough, we will use you to procreate a new generation of males who will serve us forever," he said.

"I feel like Eve in the Garden of Eden," Jenny said softly.

Asmodais laughed. "You are much stronger and more beautiful than Eve, and a lot sexier."

Then he disappeared.

Jenny felt warmth in her womb. She knew that Asmodais would take care of them.

Asmodais had two problems he had to deal with immediately. He had to get out of the cave and appear to be Asmodais Winters. He could not allow this body to be left behind and destroyed and still control the vast empire he had amassed.

It would be simple to link out of there and be gone but he needed the access of the body. He walked through the cave to a very small entrance. The women would not be able to exit this way but he could. He willed his body to be smaller and exited through the narrow area.

Asmodais reappeared at the home of Clarence Mann, one of his devoted followers, in a few seconds. His body arrived a few seconds later. Clarence Mann was a competitor in the securities business in America, and Asmodais had supplied Mann Securities with a few patents over the years to make the company stable and strong in the securities market.

"How can I help you, Master?" the rotund Clarence Mann asked as he sipped bourbon and water.

"I need you to go to Scale Mountain from the north side and retrieve Jenny Lynn and her mother. You will need some explosives to get to them, so be careful. I do not wish the young woman to be harmed," Asmodais said.

"What about her mother?" Clarence asked.

"She is of little consequence. If you can save her, then do so. Jenny Lynn is the important one. She is carrying my son," Asmodais said calmly.

"What do I do with them when I save them?" Mann asked.

"You take them to the Lynn estate. They should be safe there for a while. I want you to look in on them every few days until I call for them," Asmodais responded.

"Can I enjoy them? You do know that my son, Harvey, is in love with Jenny?" Mann said.

"They are your responsibility until I send for them. You do what is necessary for their survival. If you hurt the young woman, then nothing on this Earth will save you from my wrath. Jenny is off-limits to Harvey," Asmodais told him warningly.

"It will be as you desire. Can I do anything else for you?" Mann said calmly.

Asmodais told him he needed a car to drive to Logan Airport in Boston. Mann offered his son's blue convertible Porsche, which Asmodais accepted with a smile. Mann's wife, Melissa Mann, entered the spacious den with her nineteen-year-old daughter. Asmodais smiled at her. She had been one of his conquests twenty years early. The daughter was one of his offspring.

"I will enjoy your females before I leave," Asmodais. The two females waited as he came to them. He took their hands, and the three of them went upstairs to the master bedroom. When he returned downstairs with the daughter, Clarence Mann was gone. He left the Mann estate in the blue Porsche with Mandy Mann in the passenger seat. She would drive the car back from Logan after he finished with her. He needed to fly over the ocean to get back to Europe. He could easily have materialized at Logan Airport and been on the next flight to Paris, but then, what fun would that be? Besides, he had to lure Marsala away from the Lynn estate before Mann was able to retrieve the women.

Marsala Chases Asmodais

Marsala was on the secure telephone line to the Vatican Elite Force Command when he was informed that Asmodais Winters had been spotted on Interstate 95 heading toward Boston. He quickly packed up Samantha and Sam and headed toward Boston. He had not been on I-95 more than a few minutes when he noticed the traffic beginning to back up heavily.

Samantha quickly got onto her cell phone and called the radio station that provides continuous road condition updates for motorists. She told Marsala that a tractor-trailer carrying toxic fuel had jackknifed in Bridgeport, and everything south of the accident was at a standstill. She received an FBI alert for a blue Porsche that had run the semi off the road thirty minutes earlier.

"Asmodais is trying to delay us. He is trying to get to Logan Airport ahead of us," Marsala said, agitated.

"Stop all blue Porsches and delay them. Call me back when you have the man in custody," Samantha texted over the phone to the FBI network.

"We have to get out of this traffic!" Marsala stared at the unmoving vehicles.

"Take this exit. There are a thousand ways to get to Boston other than this route," Samantha ordered.

Marsala followed her directions and cut over to the Merritt Parkway, then took Route 8 to Waterbury, where they caught Interstate 84 toward Hartford. They were approaching Hartford some ninety minutes later when Samantha's cell phone rang.

The caller told her that the blue Porsche had eluded the roadblock after the I-91 turnoff. The vehicle must have pulled off before the Mystic Seaport exit, but the roadblocks were still in place.

Instead of turning south on I-91, Marsala was directed to continue on I-84 toward Boston. Sam, in the backseat relayed the message that the traffic was clear all the way to I-90 in Massachusetts. She had been monitoring traffic reports along the route. Sam's news was correct, and they made it to I-90 in record time. Accidents had occurred behind them on I-84, and I-91 was at a standstill.

Marsala now believed they were ahead of Asmodais and would reach the airport hours before their target, plenty of time for them to establish a plan of attack when Asmodais arrived on the scene. He felt good about his chances of catching the Prince of Lust before the man was able to leave America. He asked Sam to review all airplanes destined to Paris from the international airport.

Sam was quiet for a few minutes then announced that there were two scheduled flights to Paris the next morning, one at eight and a second flight at eleven thirty. There were also two flights to London's Heathrow Airport at nearly the same time.

They pulled into the Marriott at the airport around one in the morning and took a room for the rest of the night.

Meanwhile, Asmodais and Mandy Mann had pulled into a Marriott off exit 88 around ten at night. While the young woman prepared herself for the remainder of the night, he watched the news on the television. He smiled when the announcer reported that I-95 was still backed up and would be closed until later the next day. He hoped the VEF agent was stuck in the traffic, but even if he had been able to avoid that mess, he had caused similar accidents on I-91 and I-84. There was no way that Marsala could reach him before he reached the airport and was on the airplane to Paris.

When Mandy reappeared from the bathroom, he smiled at the beautiful dark-haired female. He'd had his choice between the mother and the daughter. He had made the right decision. He was about to bed her when a knock came to the suite door. Mandy went to the door and opened it. In walked the beautiful receptionist who had checked them in and another young woman.

Mandy looked pleased. "Master, I believe we are about to have a party." She set the alarm for five in the morning then they all went to bed.

The two hotel staffers left around four in the morning, very pregnant.

The Final Battle

Marsala sketched a picture of the android who had piloted the helicopter. He believed this android had been a duplicate of Asmodais Winters. Sam filled in the holes to give a more accurate photograph of what Asmodais Winters would look like. She had noted the pilot of the chopper too. When all three thought the picture was a good likeness of Asmodais, Sam duplicated the photographs at lightning speed. In all, they had twenty pictures to distribute to the FBI personnel whom Samantha Lee had contacted to meet them at Logan.

They headed for the international terminal, arriving on the scene shortly after five in the morning. A staff of ten FBI agents was on hand to greet them, six men and four women.

"This is a very dangerous man," Marsala said as Samantha distributed the photos to the agents. "He has no regard for human life whatsoever. He has already killed four agents in Paris, and there is no telling how many people he has killed here in America. I would like to capture him and take him back to Rome, but I am certain he will not be captured easily. Take whatever measures you deem necessary to stop him."

"This is a big airport," one of the agents said calmly.

"Yes, but he will be looking to go back to France to the safety of his security forces. He will not be delayed. We will concentrate on international traffic going to Europe," Marsala said.

"I have checked all the fares to Paris, especially those that have been booked in the past twenty-four hours. Only two first-class tickets have been purchased. The first passenger is an Adam Wong, who will be reporting to the Chinese Embassy on his arrival. The second is a Clarence Mann from New Canaan, Connecticut, who is scheduled for a security conference in Paris for a week," Sam reported.

Samantha Lee spoke up. "I have heard of Clarence Mann. He has dealings with Winterhaven Security."

"My bet is that Asmodais will be using the Mann identity. If he checks in, then we should be notified. You know your mission—now go to it," Marsala ordered.

Marsala, Samantha and Sam went to the main security office that overlooked the international departures wing of the terminal. They watched as the FBI agents took their positions around the area.

Everyone on the early flight to Paris and to London were checked twice. Marsala was certain that Asmodais had not boarded the flight. As eleven thirty approached, he told the agents to be more alert. This was the last flight to Orly for the day. He was certain Asmodais would not miss this flight.

At eleven fifteen the area began to panic. A flight carrying visitors to Rome had crashed on runway twenty-one after taking off. People swarmed to see the ball of fire outside the large windows.

Marsala knew this was his target's ploy to sneak onto the airplane. He notified the agents on duty to be very careful and maintain their surveillance on the Paris departure gate.

It was Sam who first recognized Asmodais Winters as he approached the plane from the first class lounge. How Asmodais had made it through to the lounge through the security measures was unknown, but certainly the man boarding the airplane was Asmodais Winters. Marsala also noted that he was being led to the airplane by one of the female FBI agents. He should have known better than to assign a female to such a critical area.

Asmodais had control over females. He wasn't called the Prince of Lust for no reason at all.

"He is boarding the aircraft," Marsala announced to the agents on duty.

He watched as the agents attempted to pass through the crowded departure area. "Damn," he muttered. "They are not going to get to him in time. Samantha, Sam, come on, it is up to us to stop him," he yelled.

As fast as they could run, the three of them headed through the secure passages toward the departure gate. They barely made it to the airplane before the gate was to be closed. All three leaped onto the plane, shoving a startled young steward aside.

Marsala turned toward the first-class section and sent Samantha toward business class. Something told him that Asmodais would not be flying economy class. Marsala spotted the man immediately. He was up front with the FBI female agent in the stewardesses' area, obtaining a glass of wine.

"I have you," Marsala called out as he drew his German Luger and aimed it at Asmodais.

The female FBI agent moved quickly and took a wild shot at Marsala. He had no choice but to take her out before she killed passengers on the plane. She fell.

Her gun fell from her limp hand, and Asmodais grabbed it. He turned and fired at Marsala.

Marsala felt the pain in his shoulder, but it was not his shooting shoulder. He placed his second shot between Asmodais Winters's eyes. His target crumpled to the carpet.

"You got him," Samantha said as she rushed down the opposite first-class aisle. She quickly checked Asmodais's pulse and the pulse of the FBI agent. "They are both dead," she called back to Marsala.

Marsala holstered his gun then grabbed at his wounded shoulder. Samantha came running toward him.

"Are you—"

"I'll live," he grunted.

Suddenly the first class area was filled with FBI agents, and the bodies of Asmodais and the female agent were taken away. Marsala rechecked the pulse of Asmodais as the corpse passed him on the way out of the plane. Yes, the man was dead. Obviously he had been human after all.

What no one realized was that the face of Adam Wong had changed over the last few minutes. No one had observed the spirit of Asmodais when it left Asmodais Winters and established itself in another body. Obviously, thought Asmodais, the VEF agent did not understand what manner of creature he was dealing with … or trying to deal with. Now he would never be able to present himself as Asmodais Winters. His life would be different, but not over.

Marsala and Samantha Lee Unite

Deacon Domenico Marsala reported to Interpol and specifically the Vatican Elite Force Command that the mission was over and that Asmodais Winters was no longer an issue. They congratulated him on a job well done. Then they gave him another assignment in Europe. He was to fly to England the following morning. He asked for a day or two off to recuperate, and it was granted.

"Do you really have to go so soon?" Samantha Lee asked as she nestled with him on the bed in the airport motel room. Sam, the clone, was in the corner in rest and regeneration mode.

"The Vatican Elite Force's work is never done. It is my job. I must go where they tell me to go." He squeezed her shoulders.

"Can I go with you?" she asked.

"The danger would be too great. You are not trained to fight demons and devils of this caliber," he said, knowing that his words fell on deaf ears. She had already made up her mind to go with him.

"You can teach me. I am a quick learner. You can never tell when you might need a woman to help you in your fight. Plus Sam could work with us," she said, nestling even closer to him.

"You have a job with the FBI," he reminded her.

"It would be good for my career to be the first FBI agent to team with Interpol and the VEF," she said, running her fingers across his chest.

"Yes, but could you give up the Mannys and Leroys you have cultivated so well?"

"I would give them up in a second to be with you. I have survived without them since you have been on the scene, right? Besides I have never been to England, and who knows what new friends I could cultivate over there?"

"You are impossible," he said, stretching out on the bed.

"And just think, when you are cold at night, there will always be a hot body to keep you warm, and I don't mean Sam's body!" she whispered.

"You do make a good point," he said as she pressed even closer.

"Well?" she asked, teasing him with her body. She wanted a commitment from him.

"I guess we can give it a try, but I can't promise you that the Vatican Elite Force Council will accept you as a member of my team," he said, smiling, as her lips touched his lips.

"We don't have to tell them anything just yet, do we?" she said, crawling on top of him. She now knew she was going to London with him. She would call the FBI after they were on their way to the airport. Never give your boss any more time that is absolutely necessary to make a decision. Besides she had some vacation coming anyway.

Three days later the three of them made plans for London, England, and their adventures continued.